The Happy Hollisters and the Monster Mystery

By JERRY WEST

Illustrated by Helen S. Hamilton

DOUBLEDAY & COMPANY, INC.

GARDEN CITY, NEW YORK

Contents

CHAPTER 1

A Strange Face

"THIS is a special meeting of our detective club," said Pete Hollister. "Please come to order."

The blond, crew-cut, twelve-year-old boy waited until the club members were seated on benches in the basement of the Hollister home.

"All right," Pete said finally, "you have all heard about the Shoreham monster. We're going to solve this mystery. Ann Hunter, will you please call the roll."

The club secretary stood up and read from a large notebook. "Pam Hollister."

"Here," the blond, ten-year-old girl replied.

"And I see all the other Hollisters are present," Ann Hunter went on, "Ricky, Holly, and Sue."

They sat like steps, seven, six, and four years old. Redheaded Ricky wrinkled his freckled nose. Holly twirled one of her pigtails and tickled Sue, who hunched her shoulders and giggled.

Next to reply was seven-year-old Donna Martin. She dimpled when her name was called. After that came Pete's pal, Dave Mead, and finally Jeff Hunter.

"Good, all present," said Pete. "Thank you, Ann."

The younger children wriggled and squirmed. Pete glanced out of the window into the growing darkness and called for order again. "It's kind of late already, so we'd better get right down to business," he said. "Besides the monster mystery there is also the new toy library in Washington School, you know."

"What's that?" Dave Mead asked. He was a tall boy of Pete's age.

"Pam will tell us," Pete replied.

Pam Hollister rose and smiled. "This is going to be fun," she said, and told them about a project in the grade school located in another part of town.

"They have a new kind of library there," Pam continued. "Instead of borrowing books, the children can borrow toys. I think the Shoreham Detective Club should help to find toys for the library."

"Yikes!" said Ricky. "Doesn't everybody have toys?"

"Some children don't," his sister answered. "There's not enough money to buy them."

"That's right," put in Dave. "We're just lucky. And we should help."

"But where will we get the toys?" asked dark-haired Jeff Hunter, who was eight years old.

"Ask people for them," his sister Ann replied.

"Sure," Pete said. "I know Dad will be glad to offer some from his store."

Mr. Hollister had a combination hardware and sporting-goods store in downtown Shoreham. It also included a fine toy department.

"Let's vote on it," Donna Martin suggested. She made the motion, which was seconded by Pam.

"All in favor," Pete said, "raise your right hand."

As all hands shot into the air, a terrifying shriek pierced the room. Everyone whirled to look at Holly Hollister. She stood white-faced, trembling, and pointed at the cellar window.

"I saw it! I saw the monster!" she gasped.

"What?" Pete stared at his sister.

"It just came and went!" Holly was still shaking.

"Calm down," her brother said, and went over to the window. Nothing could be seen outside but the gray sky, and the only sound was the chirping of crickets.

Pam put her arm around Holly. "Are you sure it wasn't Zip looking into the window?"

Just then the Hollisters' beautiful big collie dog padded down the steps into the basement.

"No, it wasn't Zip," Ricky declared. "He's been upstairs all the time."

Since Holly insisted that she had seen the face

7

of the Shoreham monster, Pete trotted upstairs, went out the back door, and searched around the house. Nothing!

Mr. and Mrs. Hollister were out shopping. Pete heard Domingo, their pet burro, braying from his stall in the garage. The boy quickly checked on him but found him alone. Pete patted Domingo's nose, then returned to the basement.

"Nothing out there," he said. "Did anybody else see the face?"

Nobody had.

"What did it look like?" Ricky wanted to know.

Holly frowned. "Well, it was wrinkled, like an old man, with great big teeth!"

"Yikes!" Ricky sighed. "Now we've got to look around for a little old man with big teeth!"

The others laughed, and Holly banged her brother with her elbow. "I'm not kidding!"

"Well, Pete, what are we going to do about the monster, anyway?" Dave Mead asked.

The detective club members discussed the mystery, which was being talked about all over town. Hikers had reported seeing odd footprints along the edge of a wooded trail in the State Park, which was located north of Shoreham.

The creature who had made those impressions seemed to have hoofs with three hornlike toes, and a small, delicate finger at the end of each toe.

8

"So our little old man has not only big teeth, but fingers on his toes," said Ricky.

Everyone laughed, but Pete raised his hand. "Now listen, this is serious. The whole town is scared. Some people won't even go out at night. They're afraid they might meet the monster."

Little Sue wriggled on the bench. "There aren't any monsters," she said. "Mommy told me."

"True. But something or somebody's making those funny tracks," Pete replied, and explained that other clawed prints had been seen near the shore of Pine Lake, which bordered the back yard of the Hollisters' home.

"Do you think somebody's playing a joke?" Dave asked.

"Well, that's what we have to find out," Pete declared.

All the club members agreed to join in the search. Any clues they found would be reported to Pete.

"And don't forget the toy library," Pam reminded them.

It was May, and school was nearly over. The library would be dedicated in a short time and would be open during the summer for children of the Washington School district.

After Pete had closed the meeting and the children had left, the sound of tires could be heard in the driveway outside. Four headlights shone into the window.

"Two cars," Pete said. "I wonder who's with Mother and Dad."

The children thumped up the cellar stairs, through the house, and onto the front porch. Mr. and Mrs. Hollister had parked the car and were carrying several packages inside. A tall man in uniform followed them.

"Hi, everyone!" he called out.

"Officer Cal!" Holly ran over to the policeman, who picked her up in his arms.

Officer Cal Newberry was a handsome young man with red cheeks and clear blue eyes. He belonged to the Shoreham Police Department and was a great friend of the Hollisters. He had helped them solve some of their mysteries, and they had cleared up some of his, too.

Pete glanced over at the police car and noticed a boy inside. "Who's that?" he asked.

Officer Cal turned around. "Come on out, Alex," he called. "I want you to meet some friends of mine."

From the car stepped a boy about Pete's age. He was tall, very slender, and walked with an easy motion. His skin was light brown, his black hair closely cropped, and he was dressed in dungarees, a skivvy shirt, and sneakers.

As he stepped to Officer Cal's side, a wide smile crossed his face.

"This is Alex Kane," the policeman said. "Meet the Hollisters."

Pete and Ricky shook hands with the boy, as did Mr. Hollister, a tall, handsome man.

Mrs. Hollister, slender and pretty, said, "Hello, Alex. Are you Officer Cal's assistant?"

"Sort of," Alex replied.

"He sure is," Cal Newberry smiled. "Alex was riding on his bicycle, when he saw something very unusual."

"Oh! Tell us about it!" Pam urged.

Alex said he was pedaling home from a bicycle ride in the State Park, when he had a flat tire. By the time he had repaired it, it had grown dark.

"I was going as fast as I could," the boy explained, "when suddenly I saw kind of a shadowy shape ducking behind these houses here." With a sweep of his hand he pointed to the homes located along the shore of Pine Lake. "When Officer Cal drove by," Alex concluded, "I told him about it."

"See!" Holly cried. "What did I tell you? I saw the monster's face in our window!"

The little girl quickly related the story. Then the policeman said, "Come on down to the basement, Holly, and show me where you saw the face."

Everyone including Alex went downstairs.

"It was right over there," Holly stated, and led them past the recording machine and the big box

"I've got him!" Alex yelled.

in which White Nose, the Hollisters' cat, and her five kittens were sleeping.

"That's the window!" Holly pointed up just as a blurred figure moved quickly past in the dim light.

"There it is again!" the pig-tailed girl shrieked.

Everyone raced up the stairs. The quickest of them all was Alex Kane. His long legs carried him up with the speed of an Olympic runner. He bolted out the back door and around the side of the house. Seconds later he threw himself upon a fleeing figure.

"I've got him!" he yelled, as the others hurried to the spot where he and his captive rolled over and over in the grass.

"Let me up!" a protesting voice called out. The same instant Officer Cal whipped out his flashlight. Its beam circled the two figures as they rose from the ground. Alex had collared another boy, whose face squinted in the bright light.

"Ugh!" Ricky Hollister shook his head disdainfully. "It's Joey Brill!"

CHAPTER 2

Ricky Is Trapped

"No! Joey's not the monster that I saw," Holly said.

Officer Cal smiled. "Are you sure?"

"Yes! Joey's not an old man with big teeth!"

"So what are you grabbing me for?" Joey complained, and shrugged away from Alex. He was a boy in Pete Hollister's class at Lincoln School. Large and heavy-set for his age, he used his added size to bully younger children.

Ever since the Hollisters had moved into Shoreham, Joey Brill, with his scowling face and unfriendly ways, had pestered them whenever he could. Now he was angry at being caught on their property.

"What were you doing here, Joey?" Officer Cal asked sternly. "Were you sneaking behind the houses down on the lake front?"

"No, I just got here," the boy replied. "I saw the police car and wondered what all the excitement was about. When I saw the light in the cellar, I just looked. That's all."

Alex said he could not be sure that Joey was the mysterious form he had seen lurking about.

"Well, you'd better go home, Joey," the policeman advised, and cautioned him about wandering about after dark.

"Maybe the monster will get you, Joey!" little Sue piped up, rubbing her eyes sleepily.

"No such luck," Ricky said.

"Hush!" Mrs. Hollister scolded him.

"Oh, I'll get you for that, Ricky," Joey muttered, shaking his fist at the redhead.

Mr. Hollister turned in order to hide a smile over Ricky's remark. Then he told his son not to talk fresh like that.

"Well, he's a pain," Ricky said. "Thinks he's smart because he's got some firecrackers."

"Oh?" The policeman frowned as Joey hurried off to his own home.

"That's against the law, isn't it?" asked Pam.

"Right," Officer Cal said. "Did you ever see Joey with firecrackers?"

"No, he's just bragging about 'em, I guess," Ricky replied. "I don't want to get him in any more trouble."

Just then the radio in the police car began to make a squawking noise. Cal hurried toward it and listened. "I have another call," he said. "Must go now."

He opened his trunk and pulled out Alex's bicycle. "Sorry I can't take you home, Alex."

"We'll take care of him," Mr. Hollister offered, as the policeman backed out of the driveway and sped off.

"Come in and have some milk and cookies with us," Mrs. Hollister suggested. Shy at first, Alex responded with a smile when Pete gave him a friendly pat on the back.

The Hollisters had a large kitchen with a round table and comfortable captain's chairs. Mrs. Hollister set it quickly, and the six children took their places. Each had a big glass of milk and shared a plate of cookies.

"You have a keen place over here," Alex said.

"Glad you like it," Pete replied, and told of the detective club meeting which had been interrupted by the face at the window.

"Maybe it really was the same prowler," Alex said, glancing at Holly.

"Don't worry, we'll solve the mystery," Ricky said importantly.

When Alex asked more about the club, Pam explained it.

"Man, I'd like to join, too," the boy said. "What do you have to do to get in?"

Pete replied that they used to have an initiation, which was nothing more than a few silly tricks played on the blindfolded candidate.

"Joey Brill and Will Wilson tried to get in, but they weren't brave enough." Holly giggled. Shivering a little, she added, "I guess I wasn't so brave either, tonight."

This gave Pam an idea. "I think we should make brave deeds the way to get into our detective club from now on," she suggested.

"Yes, how about that?" Pete glanced around the table.

The children eagerly agreed, all except little Sue. She had fallen asleep and was gradually sliding off the seat of the slippery chair.

Pam quickly reached her before she fell and carried her upstairs to bed.

"I'll tuck her in," Mrs. Hollister said, and Pam rejoined the others.

It was decided that if Alex should perform a brave deed, he could join the detective club.

"I think I can do that." The boy grinned broadly. "My father's very brave."

As the little party broke up, Mr. Hollister offered to drive Alex home in the station wagon.

"I live near Washington School," the boy told them.

"Where they're going to have the new toy library?" Pam asked.

"Yes," Alex replied. "My family's working on the project."

"So are we," Pam said.

Alex put his bicycle in the back of the station wagon and slid into the front seat, accompanied by Pete. It wasn't long before they stopped in front of his home, a small, neat bungalow two blocks from the school.

"Thank you, Mr. Hollister," Alex said. He took his bike out of the station wagon. "See you soon, after my brave deed!" With a grin and a wave of his hand, he disappeared into his back yard, and the Hollisters left.

The next day was Saturday, and the children decided to seek toys for the library. After a few chores were done around the house and lunch was finished, Mrs. Hollister drove her youngsters to town.

While Pam and Holly helped with the food marketing, the boys went into The Trading Post. Indy Roades met them inside the long, one-story building. It had the pleasant smell of hardware and sporting goods.

"Hi," Pete greeted his father's assistant. Indy was a real Indian from the Southwest. He was short, squat, and had a happy, tanned face.

"You want to be salesmen today?" Indy asked with a big grin.

"No, we'd like to get some toys for the new toy library," Pete replied.

"Yes, I read about that," Indy replied, as Mr. Hollister joined them.

"Here're some things ready for you," he said, and

pointed to a metal dump truck, a whistling top left over from his Christmas sale, and a box of doll dishes.

Ricky looked pleased with the truck and the top. He frowned at the doll dishes. "Who'd want to play with them?"

"Girls, of course." Mr. Hollister smiled. "I'll wrap these, and you can take them to the toy library. I hear the school will be open for contributions until two o'clock."

The boys took the toys and, after a twenty-minute walk, arrived at Washington School. It was in the center of the oldest section of town. In the rear was an asphalt-covered playground with four basketball courts laid out.

Half a dozen boys and a girl in dungarees were playing ball.

One of the boys, who had just completed a lay-up shot, turned and ran toward the Hollisters.

"Hi, Pete. Hi, Ricky."

"Hello, Alex," Pete said. "We've got some toys for the library. Dad gave them to us."

"The school is open, isn't it?" Ricky asked.

"Sure. Go in there and turn left. They're setting up the library in the storage room. My mother's there."

"Your mother?" asked Ricky.

"Yes, she's chairman. See you later."

Alex returned to the game. The ball was thrown

to him, and he dribbled it up under the basket, then sprang high in the air to sink a perfect shot. Pete and Ricky looked on for a second, then went toward the building. They climbed up half a flight of stairs, turned left, and proceeded down a long corridor to a small room.

Its walls were lined with shelves, containing many toys, and at a table in the center of the room sat two women, writing on white index cards.

"I'm Pete Hollister, and this is my brother Ricky," Pete said.

The women turned and smiled. The older one, about Mrs. Hollister's age, replied, "I'm Mrs. Kane, and this is my friend, Miss Hewitt."

"Pleased to meet you," Pete said. "We know Alex."

"Yes, he told me about your family," Mrs. Kane said. She was a plump woman and had light brown skin. Ricky noticed that her nose had a few freckles, like his.

"We have some toys for your library," Pete went on, and put the package on the table.

Miss Hewitt opened it. "Just what we need!" she exclaimed, beaming at Mrs. Kane. "Thank you very much, boys."

"We're trying to find some more, too," said Pete, waving good-by. They left and ran back to the schoolyard.

Alex saw them and threw the ball in a high arc

to Pete, who raced onto the court and began to play.

"Hey, Pete," Ricky called out, "I'm going back to The Trading Post."

"Okay. Tell Dad I'll be along soon," Pete answered, flipping the ball to his friend. Ricky lingered for a few seconds, then started to trot along the street. Soon he was back in the center of town. That dump truck his father had given to the library looked like fun, he thought. Maybe he could play with one just like it.

Just before he reached The Trading Post, he heard somebody running behind him. He turned around to meet Joey Brill face to face.

"Hey, where's everybody?" Joey asked brightly.

When Ricky told him that Pete was playing basketball behind Washington School, Joey frowned. "Over there! That's crummy!"

"They're nice kids," Ricky said stanchly.

Without replying, Joey glanced about, obviously to see if any other Hollisters were around. Then he slipped a hand into his pocket and pulled out a small red tube. At the same time he said, "Ricky, look over there—what's that?"

As the smaller boy turned about, Joey struck a match and lit the fuse of a little firecracker.

"I don't see anything, Joey—"

Bang! The firecracker exploded near Ricky's legs.

"You'll never get through there!" Joey cried.

"Ow!" the redhead cried, and gave a startled jump. "Cut that out, Joey!"

"I told you I'd get even," Joey smirked. He pushed Ricky against the wall of a building and held him with one elbow while he lighted another firecracker. Ricky squirmed free and began to run.

But Joey gave chase, passed Ricky, and cut off his way to The Trading Post. Ricky glanced about wildly. Where could he go? He saw a narrow space between two buildings, dashed toward it, and wriggled through the opening.

Joey watched him and chuckled gleefully. "You'll never get through there!" he cried, raising his hand to throw the firecracker.

"Don't!" screamed Ricky.

Joey paid no heed.

Blam! The explosion reverberated between the two buildings. As Ricky tried frantically to get out of the way, he felt himself being squeezed tighter and tighter between the two walls.

Just then a woman came by and saw what Joey had done. "Get away from there, you bad boy!" she scolded. Then she called to Ricky.

"Come on out, little boy. Over here!"

Ricky struggled, but it was impossible.

"Help!" he cried out. "Help! I'm stuck!"

CHAPTER 3

Brave Alex

"Oh! It's the Hollister boy," said another passer-by. "I'll go for his father. That poor child!"

Ricky, meanwhile, was perspiring. His heart thumped rapidly in his chest, pressed tightly against the brick wall. Would he be stuck there forever?

"Easy does it, son," came Mr. Hollister's voice. "Don't move. We'll get you out of there."

He hastened off. Two minutes later the wail of sirens filled downtown Shoreham. They moaned to a halt at the curb.

"My son's caught between the walls," Mr. Hollister told one of the firemen who came running up.

"The captain'll be right here," the man replied. At the same moment Ricky recognized the voices of Pete and Alex.

"Hey, how'd you get in there?" his brother called out.

"Sh! He shouldn't even talk," Alex warned. "He must save his strength."

Just then a fireman wearing captain's insignia

pushed through the crowd to the side of Mr. Hollister. "Don't worry," he said. "We'll get your boy out."

"Hi, Dad!" Alex shouted.

Pete looked at the man in amazement, then at Alex. "He's your father?"

"Sure."

Captain Kane was a fine-looking man. His coloring was slightly darker than Alex's, but he had the same strong face and confident manner.

The captain shouted some orders to his men, who placed a ladder against the building. Followed by a fireman with a coil of rope, he climbed to the roof and looked down on the trapped Ricky.

Captain Kane fashioned a loop and let it down. Ricky tried to reach it, but his small hands slipped from the rope.

"That won't work," said Mr. Hollister, who had climbed up beside the fire captain. "He's too weak. Can you break out the walls?"

"We could, but it might be quite a shock for your youngster. Let's try grease first."

Captain Kane called down to one of his men for a bucket of grease. A small truck roared off immediately to the Shoreham Town Maintenance Garage.

"The question is," said the captain, "how'll we get it down and smear it on the boy?"

"Dad! I'll do it!" cried Alex.

His father turned around. "What are you doing up here, son?" he asked sternly.

"I can help. I know I can," Alex replied.

Pete looked up admiringly at his new friend as Alex went on, "Let me down on a rope, Dad. I'll smear Ricky with the grease, and maybe you can pull him out that way."

"Well," Mr. Hollister said, "an adult certainly can't squeeze down between these two walls."

"I'm skinny enough," Alex urged. "Please, Dad?"

"Okay, let's give it a try."

By this time a huge crowd had gathered on the sidewalk and in the street. A police car, its dome light flashing red, pulled up, and two officers began to clear onlookers from the blocked street.

Mr. Hollister, meanwhile, talked quietly to his frightened son until the truck returned with the bucket of grease.

"Dad, can Pete Hollister come up on the roof, too?" Alex asked his father.

Mr. Kane said yes, and Alex beckoned to Pete, who followed the fireman with the bucket.

A rope sling was made and put around Alex's shoulders.

"Will he fit between the buildings?" Pete asked Captain Kane.

"Just about, with two inches to spare!"

Alex took the bucket in one hand, sucked in his

breath, and was eased carefully down to the trapped boy.

"Close your eyes tight, Ricky," he called out. "I'm going to pour some of this stuff on you."

Ricky obeyed, and the greasy glob spilled down his red hair. In a minute he was a black, gooey mess!

"I'll drop you another rope, Alex. See if you can tie it around Ricky," the fire captain ordered.

Alex maneuvered the rope under Ricky's armpits and tied it. The men on top pulled gently, but Ricky did not budge.

"Come on now, we'll try again. Easy!" Captain Kane commanded.

"Ow!" Ricky cried, as the bricks scraped his body. Then all of a sudden, like a slippery watermelon seed, the boy popped upward. The onlookers shouted as he was gently hauled to the roof.

Alex, who was almost as greasy as Ricky, was pulled up after him.

Mr. Hollister talked to his son soothingly while Captain Kane covered him with a tarpaulin and carried him on his shoulders down to the street. The others followed.

A doctor had been called and was waiting already. He looked the redhead over quickly. "A few scratches, but no harm done," he said. "Just a day's rest and he'll be all right again."

Ricky was whisked home in a police car, and Mr.

Hollister turned to Alex. "That was a very brave deed!" he said, shaking the boy's hand.

Pete slapped his new friend on the back. "It automatically makes you a member of the Shoreham Detective Club!"

"Thanks, Pete." Alex grinned. "I'd better go home and get cleaned up!"

Hearing the police car arrive, Mrs. Hollister went onto the porch. At first she did not recognize her son as he stepped from the car; then she gasped.

"Oh! Ricky!"

The three girls raced out of the house just as the station wagon with Mr. Hollister and Pete pulled in behind the police car.

"John!" Mrs. Hollister cried out. "What happened? Did he fall into an oil tank?"

Pete spilled out the story as quickly as he could and added, "Wait a minute, Mother. I'll get some detergent."

The policeman excused himself and drove off, leaving Ricky standing like a chocolate Easter bunny.

Pete came back, sloshing a bucket of warm water and a container of detergent. When the two had been mixed, Mr. Hollister lifted the pail and dribbled the water over Ricky's head. Soon the red began to show through, but Pete had to run for the fifth bucket before Ricky looked like himself again.

Then his mother said, "Come on now, into the tub!"

"I'll take care of him," Mr. Hollister said. "Will you bring me the scrubbing brush, Elaine?"

Pam and Mrs. Hollister served Ricky his supper in bed. After that he had a children's aspirin and slept soundly all night. His mother said he might be excused from church next morning, but he wouldn't hear of it.

Ricky appeared with a small limp and immediately became the hero of the day. Children crowded around to ask him about his experience. In the afternoon, he played games indoors.

By Monday morning, however, the redhead bounced out of bed and even got to school early!

Due to a teachers' conference, the children got home sooner than usual. After lunch Pete telephoned Alex, asking him to meet the rest of the detective club at police headquarters.

"We're going to get all the information possible about the monster," he said. "Everybody will be there except Dave. He's in bed with a cold."

Officer Cal was on desk duty when the club members arrived. Before him in a card catalogue was all the information about the mysterious figure seen running about Shoreham at night.

"I see here," the policeman said, "that footprints have been reported."

"Is there any real proof of this?" Donna Martin asked.

"No casts or photos," the officer replied, "but the informants are reliable people."

"We'll get proof!" Ricky piped up.

"But don't get stuck between any more buildings," Officer Cal said, ruffing Ricky's hair.

Hearing that the prints were seen at the edge of State Park, the club members decided to go there for a thorough search.

"I've got to do some deliveries for my father first, though," said Pete. "Want to come, Alex?"

"Sure thing."

Holly, Sue, and the other club members went home. Only Pam and Ann Hunter walked back to The Trading Post with the boys. They wanted to collect some more toys for the library.

"Let's visit Mr. Feinberg's store, Ann," Pam suggested on the way.

"Okay," said Pete, "I'll meet you at home around three." He waved to the girls and went on with Alex.

Mr. Jules Feinberg, who was a good friend of Mr. Hollister's, owned a specialty toy shop several blocks away. When Pam and Ann skipped into his store, he moved from behind the counter to greet them.

"Hello, girls! To what do I owe this nice visit? Did The Trading Post run out of toys?"

Pam laughed. "No. Daddy's store still has plenty of toys. But we want some from you."

"Hm." Mr. Feinberg winked at them. "Mine are better?"

Ann Hunter looked at Pam and giggled. "We want them for the library, Mr. Feinberg."

The man looked puzzled. "You mean books. Like Nancy Drew and the Hardy Boys."

Pam explained that they were talking about a toy library, and the merchant's eyes widened. "Say, that's a fine idea," he said. "I'll be glad to donate something. How about a doll for a girl, and this helicopter here for a boy?"

"Does it really fly?" asked Ann.

"Of course. You wind it up like this. Watch!"

Mr. Feinberg turned a key and wound up the helicopter. When he released it, it made a loud rackety sound and rose into the air.

"That's keen," Pam exclaimed, as the storekeeper let the helicopter run down and put it in a box. "And look at this nice Raggedy Ann doll."

Beaming with delight, the girls took the toys, thanked Mr. Feinberg, and hastened out of the store.

"Mrs. Kane will love to get these," Pam said. The two girls waited for a green light to cross the street, when a boy walked up beside Ann Hunter. Pam saw him first and whispered, "Here comes Will Wilson. Watch out."

"You wind it up like this. Watch!"

"Hey, did you see Joey?" Will asked.

"No," Ann replied.

"Well, if you—what have you got there?" The boy turned his head sideways to look at the box. "Oh, a helicopter—just a fake one, I guess."

"It really works," Ann said. "Mr. Feinberg showed us."

Will Wilson was a friend of Joey Brill's. He often joined him in pestering the Hollisters.

"What does a girl want with a helicopter?" Will went on. The light turned, and they started across the street.

Suddenly Will punched the box out from under Pam's arm. He caught it before it hit the street. Then he flew off like an arrow.

"Come back, Will Wilson!" Ann cried out. "Give us back that helicopter!"

CHAPTER 4

Fake Footprints

THE two girls chased Will Wilson. Pam started to gain on the boy, when suddenly he turned around a corner to where his bicycle was parked by the curb.

"Stop, you meanie!" Pam cried out. Will started off, holding the box in his left arm and steering with his right. At first he wobbled down the street, and Pam barely missed grabbing his shirt.

"We won't let him get away with this!" Ann Hunter exclaimed hotly.

"You bet we won't!"

"We know where he lives," Ann said. "Come on, let's tell his mother."

The girls hastened through the downtown area. Presently the stores gave way to a pleasant section of small houses along tree-lined streets. Although the back yards were small, they were neatly kept, many of them having little flower gardens.

"He lives right down there," Pam said, and pointed to Will Wilson's place. They ran up the walk to the front door. Pam pushed the bell outside the screen door. She could hear it buzz in the kitchen.

A thin little woman appeared and gazed over the top of her eyeglasses at the two callers.

"Are you Mrs. Wilson?" asked Pam politely.

"Yes. But I don't want any Girl Scout cookies today."

Pam smiled and said, "We're not selling anything. We just want to get our helicopter."

"Dear me! What happened, did it fly away?"

"No. Will took it!" Ann Hunter put in. "It was for the Washington School toy library."

"Where's Will, did he come home with it?" Pam went on.

Mrs. Wilson looked annoyed. "I don't know what you want, but I have a load in the washing machine. Can you come back later?"

"Please, Mrs. Wilson," Pam urged, "we have to find Will!"

"Goodness!" The woman sighed, and the girls could see she was exasperated. "Will gets into more trouble since he's been playing with that Brill boy." Then she wiped several strands of hair from her forehead and looked at Pam. "Will rode past the house a few minutes ago. He was headed toward Joey Brill's."

"Did he have a box in his hand?"

The woman nodded. "If it's yours, tell Will I said to give it back."

The girls thanked Mrs. Wilson and hurried off.

Joey's house was on the other side of the street. Before they could knock on the door, a boy rode along the sidewalk and stopped. "Looking for Joey Brill?"

"Yes," Pam said. "Did you see him?"

"He and Will are riding up to the State Park. Asked me to go along and watch them fly their new helicopter in the Great Meadow."

"Thank you," Pam said. Then the girls hurried on to the Hollister home.

"Oh, I hope they don't wreck that nice helicopter," Ann worried. "Let's tell your brother."

Pete and Alex, meanwhile, had finished the deliveries. When they heard what had happened, Pete said, "That sounds like a Wilson trick! Come on, we'll ride to the State Park. You girls stay home. We can handle this thing ourselves."

After half an hour of hard pedaling they drove through the stone portals of State Park, which was a favorite with the Shoreham people and other residents for miles around.

The Hollisters liked it especially as a picnic spot and often had cookouts in the large recreation area.

The roadway entered into a valley. Pine-covered slopes rose gently on either side, and in the middle

36

lay a wide, grassy playfield known as the Great
Meadow.

Far away, in the center of the meadow, Pete saw
two bicycles lying on their sides. Nearby Joey and
Will were playing with the toy helicopter.

"Let's get 'em!" Alex said, leaning over his handle
bars for greater speed.

"No, wait! If they see us, they have a head start
and might get away." Pete advised hiding their bicycles among the trees and sneaking up.

Alex agreed. They dismounted and pushed their
bikes into a dense stand of spruce trees.

Suddenly they heard a snorting sound. Something was crashing through the bushes about ten
yards away!

"Oh, oh," Pete whispered. "What's that, a deer?"
The boys followed the sound. They could see nothing in the dense underbrush but still heard the snorting and the sound of a thrashing animal.

"Let's not get too far away from the bikes," Alex
warned after a while, "or we won't find our way
back!"

They paused and looked around. The sounds had
stopped, and there was no sign of an animal.

"Come on, Pete, we've got to get that helicopter."

The boys turned and went back in a small gully.
The ground was mushy and soggy from the recent

"Man, the three-toed monster!"

rain. Suddenly Pete stopped short. "Alex! Look at this!"

In the soft ground were several deep imprints!

"Man, the three-toed monster!" Alex gasped.

"And look at these other marks, like thin fingers! They're sticking out from the sides of the hoofs."

"Nobody would believe it if they didn't see it!" said Alex.

"Look, we've got to get a plaster cast of a good print," Pete decided. "Alex, remember that telephone booth we saw at the park entrance?"

His friend nodded.

"Go there and phone my house, while I stand guard here."

"What about Joey and Will?"

"They're not as important as these prints. You know, as detectives we have to get evidence. We're hot on the trail of the monster!"

"Who do you want me to speak to?"

"Pam. Tell her to bring some hair spray, a coffee can of plaster, and a quart of water. She knows where the plaster is."

The Hollister children knew how to make molds of footprints. Officer Cal had taught them, and it often came in handy when they worked on their detective cases.

Alex disappeared quickly through the woods, while Pete remained to guard the prints. All was silent now, and the sun was getting lower in the sky. Pete hoped his sister would arrive before it got too dim in the pine forest.

To the boy's surprise, Alex and Pam appeared much sooner than expected.

"Mother drove me up in the station wagon," Pam explained. "She's waiting for us at the park entrance. Pete, did you really find the monster's footprints?"

"These might be the ones," the boy said, as he quickly set about to make the molds. While Alex watched closely, he squirted hair spray into the impression and let it dry for a few minutes. Meanwhile, he mixed the plaster and water until it was a runny, white mass. Then he poured the mixture into the prints.

"This ought to do it," he said. "Now we'll have to let it set and harden."

"What about Joey and Will?" asked Pam.

"I'll see if they're still in the meadow," Alex volunteered, and dashed off. He was back in a few minutes. "They're gone!"

"Don't worry, we'll still get the helicopter," Pete said.

By now the plaster had set long enough, and Pete pried it from the footprint.

"Crickets, this is a beauty!" he said. "I wonder what the monster itself looks like."

They returned to the car, stowed their bikes in

the back, and set off. Mrs. Hollister dropped Alex off first.

"So long," he said, waving. "And thanks for the ride. Will you come over and visit us sometime?"

"How about tomorrow?" Pete suggested. "After we take the cast to Officer Cal at headquarters."

Alex gave the okay sign and ran into his house.

The Hollisters were so excited about finding the footprints that they could hardly keep their minds on school the next day. After classes they hurried home and rode their bikes to police headquarters. Pete carried Sue in his handle-bar basket. Inside they showed the cast to Officer Cal.

"Boy, this is a clear-looking job," he praised Pete. "Tell you what. The captain knows a lot about prints. He studied for a while to be a zoologist. I'll let him have a look at it."

The youngsters waited until Officer Cal returned from an inner office. "Well, the captain is stunned," he reported. "He thought the three-toed prints might belong to a hippopotamus. But whoever heard of a hippo in the State Park? And it would have to be a midget one at that."

Cal Newberry asked Pete to leave the evidence there to assist the department.

"Sure, glad to," the boy replied. "That's what the Shoreham Detective Club is for, Officer Cal." Then he told the policeman about the toy helicopter.

"You say Will Wilson still has it?"

"Yes," Pam said. "Could you get it back for us?"

"Sure. You ride your bikes over to the Wilson house. I'll meet you there."

Just as they pulled up in front of the place, Officer Cal arrived in his car. With the others trailing behind him, he went up the steps and rang the doorbell. Will himself answered. Behind him appeared Joey Brill. His eyebrows shot up, and his face sagged in surprise.

"All right, Will," Officer Cal said sternly. "Where's the helicopter you took from Ann Hunter?"

"In-inside," Will stammered. He hastened into the house and returned with the toy in its box.

"We were only borrowing it," Joey came to his defense, "and were just about to take it back."

The policeman took the box, turned to go, but looked back over his shoulder.

"Joey," he said slowly, "did you two make those hoof prints in the State Park?"

A light came into the bully's eyes. "Maybe yes, maybe no," he quipped defiantly, then ducked into the house as fast as he could.

"I don't think he has anything to do with this," Pete said on the way down the steps.

"Don't be too sure," Ricky piped up.

After thanking Cal, the children drove up one street and down another until they came to the

42

Washington School section. They found Alex playing in the schoolyard.

"Hi," he called, and ran over to them. "Come on, I'll show you my house. Glad you could come."

The children went down the street and stopped in front of the Kane house.

"Let's go in the back," Alex said, and led the way into a neat patch of lawn edged by two gardens. Flowers were growing in one. The other contained a row of lettuce, one of tomatoes, and a third of little sprouts.

"Those are my dad's Kentucky wonder beans," Alex explained. "Man, do they ever grow high!"

Just then Mrs. Kane came out on the back porch. She looked at her son sternly. "Alex," she asked, "did you eat the custard? If you did, you could at least have used a spoon!"

CHAPTER 5

Pancake Sue

"WHAT custard?" Alex asked, surprised. "I didn't eat any custard!"

"It was cooling in a bowl right here on the porch," said his mother. "I made your favorite kind with lots of eggs."

"Maybe a dog or something ate it," said Holly.

"Oh, no," replied Mrs. Kane. "It was too high up."

As she spoke, the screen door opened and Captain Kane came out. "Well, did you solve the great custard mystery?" he asked cheerfully.

"Not yet, dear, but we will," his wife said, looking straight at Alex.

Captain Kane kissed her on the cheek. "See you later. I'm off for work."

"Are you going to the firehouse?" Ricky asked.

"We've never been there," Sue chirped.

The fire captain cocked his head. "Really? Well, come along. Alex and I will give you a quick tour."

"Crickets, that'd be keen!" said Pete, and the

44

children piled into the Kane car. Ten minutes later the captain parked in the lot behind the engine house. He took the children through a back door into a garage with two big old-fashioned fire engines in it. Both had torn leather seats.

"Gee, they look kind of crummy," Ricky piped up.

"Well, they're old, and we don't use them any more," replied Captain Kane. "As a matter of fact, they're for sale. Want one?"

"Oh, yes!" exclaimed Holly. "How much do they cost?"

The man laughed. "When your daddy is ready to buy, we'll talk it over. Here, come into the radio room."

He led the way into a large room. There a young man sat at a switchboard surrounded by other equipment, including a microphone. He looked up and smiled.

"Jim, meet the Hollisters," said Captain Kane.

Pete walked up to the man curiously. "If people want to report a fire, they call in here?"

"Right. I take their name, phone number, and the address of the fire."

"I'll bet you get a lot of excited calls," Pam said.

"Well, I try to calm them down," replied Jim. "Firemen have to stay calm to do their job, you know."

Captain Kane chuckled. "There's plenty of action

out front when that alarm bell rings. Then every-thing happens at once."

"Yeah!" Alex put in. "Twelve men on three trucks go out of here so fast it makes your head spin. Anybody gets caught in that rush'll be mashed!"

"Mashed!" said Sue, her eyes getting big.

"Flat as a pancake," said Alex.

His father led them through another door into the big main room.

"Wow! Look at that!" cried Ricky. A huge red engine stood before them with a long metal ladder lying on top of it.

"That's an aerial hook and ladder wagon," ex-plained Captain Kane. "That big baby on the top works by electricity. It unfolds and rises way up into the air, so we can climb to the top of high build-ings."

He pointed to another truck beside it. "That's a pumping engine. And that big square truck up front by the door is the rescue-squad car. It carries every-thing from life nets and gas masks to a little saw we use to cut rings off people whose fingers have got too fat."

"You're fooling us," Holly said.

"No, really!"

As the girls giggled, the captain opened a cup-board and took a white plastic fireman's hat from a hook. "Somebody want to try it on?"

"Me!" cried Ricky. "Watch out now, everybody! I'm a fire chief!" He stuck out his chest and clapped the hat on his head. "Hey, I can't see where I'm going!" he said, flopping around.

"You're a silly fire chief!" said Holly, and pulled the hat off her brother.

"Now show 'em the one-way elevator, Dad!" exclaimed Alex. He pointed to a thick shiny brass pole, which ran up through a hole in the ceiling. "One way—down only!"

The Hollisters laughed. "Can we slide on it?" Holly asked.

The captain nodded. "Alex, you take 'em upstairs and show 'em how. I'll stand below, just in case."

The children followed the boy up a long flight of stairs and down a hallway. "Here's my dad's room," Alex said. "When he's on duty at night, he sleeps here."

The children looked into the room and saw a desk with a single bed beside it. On the floor in front of the door was a brown sweater. Alex stepped over it and invited them in.

Holly twirled her pigtails. "What a mess," she chuckled. "Everything's lying on the floor!"

The fire captain's pants were lying next to the bed, with the legs still in the boots.

Pam bent down to pick them up, when all at once she heard a deep voice behind her.

"Young lady, put them right back!"

Pam whirled around to see a tall fireman. He gave her a little smile. "You'll see a lot of clothes lying around in certain places. That's so we can pick 'em up fast."

"See?" said Ricky, as if he knew all about it. "Firemen aren't sloppy. They're just smart."

"I suppose that's why you leave your pajamas on the bathroom floor," Pete teased his brother.

"Now seriously," Alex said. "If an alarm comes, Dad jumps out of bed into his pants and boots all at once. As he's running for the door, he picks up the sweater. Downstairs he grabs his coat and hat and *zowie!* He's gone!"

Alex then led them into a large recreation room where half a dozen firemen were sitting. Next to it was a dormitory with rows of neatly made beds. In a corner was the brass pole coming up through a hole in the floor.

Alex grabbed the pole. "Like this," he explained. "You lean one leg against it and wrap the other around. Then hang on tight and down you go!" He pulled back. "Who's first?"

"I'll go," Pete offered. He did just as Alex had said and swished down.

"Good slide!" Captain Kane called up through the hole. "I think you all can make it."

Pam followed, then Ricky, and Holly, who said,

"Sue! Slide down!"

"Whee! It's a breeze!" as her feet touched the floor below.

Alex held Sue until she had grasped the pole and her chubby legs were wrapped tightly around it.

"Hang on now, Sue," he cautioned, and let her go. The little girl held on firmly. "It's fun," she called, coming down little by little.

Suddenly the firehouse alarm bell rang with a shrill, piercing clang! Sue clung even tighter to the pole, too scared to move!

"Hurry up, Sue, slide down!" yelled Alex.

"I can't! I can't!"

Firemen raced to the pole, but Sue was in their way. Captain Kane acted quickly. He shinned up the slippery pipe and wrapped an arm around the little girl.

"Okay, sweetheart," he said kindly. "Let go!"

Sue obeyed and the next moment landed safely at the bottom. As Captain Kane swung her out of the way, the firemen came zipping down, one after the other. They leaped on the fire engines.

The front doors rolled up automatically, and the apparatus roared out into the street.

"Crickets!" Pete exclaimed. "We nearly ruined everything!"

"Sue, why wouldn't you come down?" asked Pam, giving her sister a little hug.

"'Cause I didn't want to be a pancake," sniffled

Sue. "Alex said you might get mashed flat when the bell rings!"

Alex had run into the dispatcher's room, and raced back again. "Hey, Pete!" he cried. "The fire's in your neighborhood!"

CHAPTER 6

Mystery Man

"OH no!" Pam said with a frightened look. "I hope it isn't our place."

"Wow!" cried Ricky. "Let's go!"

They raced out of the firehouse but realized then that their bikes were at Alex's.

"To The Trading Post!" commanded Pete. "Maybe Indy can take us."

Mr. Hollister and his assistant had just stepped outside the store when the children arrived.

"Must be some fire!" Indy said, looking after the disappearing engines.

"And it's in our neighborhood!" cried Pete. "Alex said so. Dad, can Indy drive us there, please?"

"Okay. The truck's out back. Hop in!"

With Pam carrying Sue, the youngsters scrambled into the pickup. Indy glanced back to see that all were seated before zipping after the fading sirens.

It took only moments for The Trading Post truck to reach the residential area of town near the lake. Now the sirens moaned lower and lower. Indy

52

caught up with the engines as they turned into the street where Joey Brill lived.

All eyes popped at what they saw. "Look!" shrilled Holly. "Joey's house is on fire!"

Smoke was billowing from an upstairs window of the Brill home. The engines clanged to a halt. Three firemen ran to a nearby hydrant, trailing hose. Two others raced inside with foam tanks on their backs.

But the most amazing sight was the Brills themselves! On the front step Mr. Brill had Joey over his knees, spanking him hard. Mrs. Brill stood by, scolding her yowling son.

"Yikes! Is he getting it!" exclaimed Ricky.

"Let's find out what happened," said Pete.

They ran over to join onlookers who had crowded around the house. Ann Hunter was among them. "Joey lit a firecracker in his room," she reported. "He was going to throw it out the window, but it caught in the curtains."

A fireman ordered everybody to move off, as another held a hose and squirted water into the window from the outside.

Soon Captain Kane's voice boomed from upstairs, "Okay, turn it off now. All out!"

"Let's go," urged Indy. "There's nothing more to look at."

"I want to see if Joey gets spanked some more," Ricky said.

"Oh, come on," Pam said, taking him by the

"Yikes! Is he getting it!"

hand. "Joey's got trouble enough without your laughing at him."

Indy drove to Alex's place for the bikes and let him off before delivering all the Hollisters to their home at the lake front.

At the dinner table that night everyone talked about the fire until Pete finally brought the conversation back to the monster.

"Let's go to the State Park tomorrow," he said to Pam. "Maybe we can pick up some clues to add to the footprints."

Just before the children went to bed, it started to rain.

"We might as well stay home," Pam said, discouraged. "The rain will wash away all clues for sure."

"Maybe there'll be *new* prints," Holly suggested, crawling under her blanket.

"Poor old monster," said Sue, yawning, "out in the rain all by himself."

Next morning it was bright and sunny. In school Pete found out that Dave Mead was still home with a cold.

"Too bad," he said to Pam on the way home. "We could have used him on our hunt today."

"Well, maybe Alex can come," she replied.

But it turned out that Alex had chores to do and couldn't join them either, so Pam and Pete set out for the State Park together.

Their bicycles hummed along in good time. Soon they turned off the main road and down a path.

"Pretty muddy," Pete stated. "We'd better leave the bikes here."

They dragged their bicycles out of sight and put them under a tree.

"Let's cut through the woods to that place where we made the mold," Pam suggested. "It's not far."

Staying parallel to the path, the two children started through the dense underbrush. It was gloomy, and only a few shafts of weak sunlight filtered through the trees. The leaves and ground were still wet from the heavy rain.

Pete and Pam surveyed the ground thoroughly as they walked along but saw no traces of the monster. Suddenly Pete froze in his tracks. He motioned to his sister and turned around.

"I thought I heard something," he whispered.

Both children held their breath and eyed the glistening underbrush. A squirrel streaked up a tree, but otherwise all was silent.

Pete shrugged. "Guess I was wrong."

Quietly they moved on, picking their way carefully over some fallen branches.

Again a sound! This time it was a soft crackling. Pam gave a stifled cry.

Peering over a bush was a small, sallow-skinned man! He had slanted eyes, and his hair was black and shiny.

The man spoke first, in a thin, singsong voice. "What are you looking for, may I ask?"

Pete and Pam stared at him, speechless. When the stranger stepped out into the open, they saw that he was short and thin and wore a tan, lightweight suit.

"Don't be afraid," he said with a funny, lopsided smile. "You are seeking the monster?"

"Wh-who are you?" Pete stammered. But before the man could reply, a shrill whistle pierced the air.

"Hey, Pete!" came Alex's voice.

The Hollisters whirled around to see their friend running toward them.

"I got finished early, so I thought I'd—"

Pete motioned Alex closer, and in a hoarse whisper he said, "L-look at that man!"

He pointed to the spot where the stranger had stood. *He was gone!*

"Man!" sighed Alex. "You're dreaming!"

"He was for real," Pam insisted. "A little fellow in a light brown suit."

"Sure. He was six inches tall and had long pointy ears."

Pete paid no attention to the joke but grabbed his sister's arm. "Come on! He's got to be someplace!"

As they looked behind bushes and trees, Alex suddenly realized that the Hollisters were serious.

57

"Who was he?" Alex asked, puzzled.

Pete shrugged. "I've no idea. He scared the daylights out of us, popping up that way."

"Do you think he was the monster?"

"Hardly." Pete grinned. "But he could be the one who's playing a joke, though."

"Well, for now let's just call him the mystery man," Pam said.

"That makes two of 'em," remarked Alex. "There's another one waiting at your house to see you. I never met such a big guy. He must be six feet ten!"

"I wonder what he wants," Pam mused.

"There's one way to find out," Pete replied. "Let's travel!"

The three hurried to their bicycles and pedaled fast for home. Near the edge of town they suddenly saw Joey and Will on their bikes lazily circling a large puddle in the center of the street.

"Oh, no!" exclaimed Pam. "That's all we need!"

"Look who's coming!" Joey sneered.

"They're in such a hurry!" called Will. "Where're you going?"

"Never mind. Get out of the way!" Alex shouted.

But Will pulled his bike across their path, hopped down, and stood astraddle. Joey was right behind him. "Stop!" he yelled.

Pete thought fast. "Gangway!" he called, and

with Pam and Alex right behind him, he swerved around Will and splashed through the puddle.

The bullies howled as the water sprayed over them.

"I'll get you!" Will yelled furiously. He jumped on his bike and made a fast turn into the puddle. But his wheels skidded. "*Yow!*" he cried, and fell sidewise into the muddy water!

CHAPTER 7

Flying Saucers

JOEY BRILL started in pursuit of Pete, Pam, and Alex. But he changed his mind and went back to his pal Will, who stood beside his bike, trying to shake some of the water from his trousers.

The Hollisters and their friend rode on steadily, avoiding puddles of water in the road. Pam was the most curious about the unknown caller who was waiting for them. "Perhaps he has something to do with the new toy library," she said.

"Or maybe he's a newspaper reporter," Alex ventured.

"We must get there before he leaves," said Pam. She increased her speed, but the sudden pressure on the pedals resulted in a clanking sound. Pam knew instantly what had happened. Her bicycle chain had broken!

She stopped to look at the chain, which was tangled up in the spokes of the rear wheel. "Just when we were in such a hurry!" she declared with a sigh.

Pete and Alex turned about and dismounted alongside the disabled bicycle. Pete freed the chain and tossed it into his handle-bar basket.

"You go on ahead," Pam said. "I'll walk the rest of the way."

Before Pete had a chance to reply, Alex was standing in the middle of the road waving down a delivery truck coming toward him. The driver stopped and leaned out the window. "Something wrong?"

Alex explained what had happened and asked the man if he had a piece of rope to spare.

The trucker flipped open a dash panel and pulled out a loop of heavy twine.

"I think this will do you," he said. "Pretty tough. It won't break."

Alex thanked the man, then turned to Pam. "Here's where you get a free ride!" He threaded the twine behind the front fork, then tied either end to the back of the other two bicycles.

Pam hopped on, and the boys pedaled off, slow at first so as not to snap the cord.

Pam had a good time being towed rapidly down the highway. Her blond hair blew in the breeze. "I feel like I'm a chariot and you're the two horses!" she sang out.

When the three entered the Hollister drive, they saw a strange car parked there.

"I'm a chariot and you're the horses!"

"I'm glad he hasn't gone yet," said Pam, adjusting her kick stand.

"That's good," Alex said. "But look, I can't go in with you. I promised my mother I'd cut the back lawn. So long now."

Alex pedaled off, and Pete and Pam hastened into the house. In the living room they found their mother talking to a man. When he rose to greet them, Pete and Pam marveled at his size. Alex was right. The man looked to be well over six feet. His hair was gray at the temples, and he wore heavy, dark-rimmed glasses. He was dressed in khaki trousers, open sport shirt, and a large, brass, monogrammed belt buckle.

"Children, this is Mr. Edward Baker," said Mrs. Hollister. "He has come all the way from New York to talk with you."

"Hello, Mr. Baker," said Pam, and Pete extended his hand. In an instant it was completely covered in Mr. Baker's huge grip. He smiled at them, then sat down again.

"So these are your detectives."

"Yes," Mrs. Hollister went on. "They're spending a lot of time on the monster mystery."

"The monster!" Pete exclaimed. "Is that what you're here for, Mr. Baker?"

The man's eyes crinkled when he smiled. "Well, just say that I'm an investigator, too, but I don't want you to start quizzing me. I can't tell you anything about my job—other than to say that I've been assigned to look for your monster."

"Crickets!" Pete said. "This case is getting more important all the time."

"It certainly is," the tall man replied, "and the detective club can be a great help to me."

Mr. Baker listened to Pete and Pam as they told him everything they knew.

"Making a cast of that footprint was very clever," Mr. Baker praised them. "It may go a long way in finding the monster. Do you know of anything else mysterious that has been going on around here?"

The youngsters thought for a few moments. Pam said, "Joey's house caught on fire, but that's no mystery. And somebody ate Mrs. Kane's custard on the back porch."

"What was that you said about custard?"

"Oh, I guess it isn't much to go on," Pam replied. "Some very hungry child must have eaten the whole bowl of dessert with his fingers."

Mr. Baker took his small notebook from his pocket and wrote something in it.

Pete smiled at him. "Is Mrs. Kane's pudding really a clue?"

"Maybe yes, maybe no." The investigator rose from his chair.

"Won't you stay to supper with us?" Mrs. Hollister said. "I would like you to meet my husband."

"Another time, perhaps," their caller said. He

turned to the children. "Well, I think I have all the information now—the face at the cellar window, the tracks in the woods, the sounds in the underbrush, and the mysterious little man you saw."

"And don't forget the custard," said Pam with a giggle.

"Oh, no. I have that in my book." Mr. Baker returned the smile and added, "I'm staying at the Lakeview Motel and will be there for a few days. Please contact me if you learn anything more."

"We just passed your place awhile ago," said Pete. "Pam's bike chain broke right near there."

"Let me look at that chain," Mr. Baker said.

He went outside with the youngsters, and Pete showed him the broken part.

"I'll fix it for you," the big man volunteered. "Where're your tools?"

"In the garage," Pete said.

When they walked inside to the workbench, Mr. Baker was amazed to see their burro, Domingo.

"Oh, we got him out West one time," Pete explained. "He's a lot of fun."

"I'm glad you like animals," the investigator said. He patted Domingo before picking out several tools.

Pam wheeled her bicycle into the garage, and Mr. Baker had it repaired in no time at all. Then he shook hands with the two children, entered his car, and drove away.

Inside, Mrs. Hollister said, "I think Mr. Baker is almost as mysterious as the monster."

"Did he tell you who he is working for?" asked Pam.

"No, he didn't."

"Well, I trust him anyhow," Pam said. "He likes animals."

Just as Pete and Pam were finishing their homework that evening, the telephone rang. It was Joey Brill.

"What do you want, Joey?" asked Pete.

"I had some news to tell you," Joey said with an air of great importance. "But you wouldn't stop to listen."

"All right," Pete said. "Tell me now."

"No, I won't," Joey replied. "You missed your chance. You'll be the *last* to know about it."

In spite of himself, Pete's curiosity was aroused. "Has it something to do with the monster?"

Joey laughed so loud that Pam could hear him clear across the room.

"So now you want to know!" Joey sneered. "Well, you'll read all about it in the newspaper tomorrow." With that he hung up.

When Pete told Pam about the call, she shrugged. "He's probably only kidding," she said.

"I don't know, Pam. He may have found out something very important."

In school the next morning, Joey Brill and Will

Wilson did not say a word to Pete; they just sat, grinning at him whenever they could.

"I wonder what they are up to," Pete thought. It wasn't until after lunch, however, that he found out. Returning to his class he saw a group of pupils crowding about the two bullies. Even the teacher was smiling at the pair.

"You're quite sure that's what you saw?" Miss Hanson asked them.

Joey Brill basked in the attention, and Pete had never seen him look so pleasant.

"Of course, everything is true," he said importantly. "Right, Will?"

Will Wilson raised his hand as if taking an oath. "And it just shows we're smarter than all the Hollisters put together," he declared.

Pete didn't know what to make of it. Feeling a little embarrassed, he approached the boys. "Say, fellows, what's all this about?"

"Oh, haven't you heard?" Miss Hanson said, and thrust a newspaper toward Pete. The headlines made him feel dizzy. In large bold type it read: FLYING SAUCERS REPORTED BY SHOREHAM BOYS. In smaller type it went on: *Think Shoreham monster may be creature from outer space.*

Pete was stunned. He gazed at the story and a large picture showing a blurred object over Pine Lake. Joey and Will, it said in the article, had Joey's camera with them and had had enough presence of mind to photograph the phenomenon.

Joey went on to the murmuring crowd about him. "We saw this thing land on the lake shore, and something crawled out of it."

"Yeah," Will continued. "Then there was a blinding flash and it disappeared."

"There aren't any such things as flying saucers," Pete said.

All the other children laughed at him. Even his teacher said, "We can't be too sure about that, Pete."

Now the bell rang and the pupils took their seats. As Joey passed Pete, he said in a loud voice, "I wouldn't join your old detective club even if you made me an honorary member!"

Pete was angry. "Why does everybody believe that fake?" he thought.

By the time school was over that afternoon, everyone knew about the famous exploits of Joey and Will, and when Mr. Hollister returned from The Trading Post at suppertime, he talked about the strange event with his wife and children.

"Half of Shoreham actually believes the story," he said, shaking his head.

"Could that photograph have been touched up in some way?" asked Mrs. Hollister.

"I don't think the newspaper would do that," Mr. Hollister replied. "They're honest people."

"But Joey and Will could have done it!" Ricky piped up, and wiggled his eyebrows.

After supper the younger children went out to play by the lake front. Holly jumped into their rowboat and paddled among the cattails looking for frogs. Ricky sat on the dock with his fishing pole, waiting for a bite. A sunfish nibbled and the cork hopped up and down, but the sunfish wouldn't take the hook.

Ricky concentrated hard for a while, then looked up. Suddenly he gaped with surprise. He dropped his pole and raced toward the house.

"I saw it!" he yelled as he jumped up the steps. "Daddy, I saw it!"

CHAPTER 8

A Prize Doll

Mr. Hollister opened the door. "What in the world—"

"It was a flying saucer!" Ricky cried out. "I saw it land on the lake!"

"Ricky saw a flying sausage!" said Sue, dancing up and down with excitement.

Mr. Hollister took his son by the hand, led him into the living room, and sat the boy on his lap. "Now, Ricky," he said. "I don't want you telling any fibs. Just exactly what did you see?"

All but Holly, who was still catching frogs, crowded around the redhead. Ricky was all out of breath.

"You see, I was fishing for sunnies and watched the cork jiggle up and down and then I looked out on the lake—and there it was! A big flying saucer, just landing on the water!"

"Maybe it was only a turtle," Pete suggested.

"Oh, no, it wasn't," Ricky insisted. "It was bigger than our boat!"

Just then the Hollisters heard their rowboat bump against the dock. Holly raced across the grass and into the house. She stopped at the door, surprised to see everyone standing around Ricky.

"Guess what I saw!" she blurted out.

"A flying sausage," chirped Sue. "Ricky saw it, too."

Holly wrinkled her nose and twirled a pigtail with her left forefinger. Suddenly she thrust her right hand in front of Mr. Hollister's face. In it was a large tadpole, with legs and a tail.

"This is my monster," declared Holly proudly.

Everyone laughed, and Mrs. Hollister said, "That tadpole will be a frog tomorrow, if you'll let him be."

"Okay." Holly turned to run back to the lake but hesitated. "What's Ricky sitting on your lap for, Daddy? Are you going to spank him?"

Ricky replied, "I was just telling him about the flying saucer *I saw!*"

"Boy, you're dreaming," Holly said, and hastened back to the dock. There she dropped the creature into the water. "Good-by, tad-frog," she said. "Mother says you'll grow up tomorrow."

Even though nobody at home believed Ricky's story about the flying saucer, his classmates at school did. *They all believed him!*

Even Joey Brill. To Ricky's great surprise, the bully put his arm around his shoulder, as if they

71

were old chums, and kept saying, "Sure, sure. What you describe is exactly what I saw."

Pete and Pam didn't know what to do about their brother. "It must have been some kind of—illusion," Pam whispered.

"Maybe the sun was shining in his eyes, or something," Pete said. "Crickets! I hope this doesn't get back to the newspapers and they start quoting Ricky."

But that was exactly what happened. Ricky's report spread quickly through Shoreham. The newspapers carried a new headline: ANOTHER BOY SEES FLYING SAUCER. IS PINE LAKE A HAVEN FOR CREATURES FROM OUTER SPACE?

The greatest shock came that evening when the family was watching the news on TV. The announcer told about the Shoreham monster and the flying saucers, giving credit to Joey, Will, and Ricky by name.

"Did you hear that?" Ricky said, and did a handspring in the middle of the living room rug.

"You're an awful ham," Pam said. "Wait until they find out you were just seeing things, Ricky."

When the program was over, Mr. Hollister picked up his newspaper and said with a smile, "At least the monster has put Shoreham on the map."

The next day was Saturday. After breakfast Pam received a telephone call from a woman who introduced herself as Mrs. Elder. She lived about a half mile up the road. "Isn't it terrible about the flying saucers and those creatures?" Mrs. Elder said. Without waiting for Pam's comment, she added, "But that's not what I called about." The woman explained that she had a beautiful Viennese doll to contribute to the toy library.

"Gracious knows I'm too old to play with it," she said. "I just love to look at the doll once in a while. However, perhaps some child can enjoy playing with this lovely toy. Would you come and get it, Pam?"

"Oh, yes," Pam replied. "This afternoon, Mrs. Elder. And thank you."

After their morning chores around the house were finished, they had a delicious lunch of roast beef sandwiches. Then Pam and Holly walked to Mrs. Elder's home. She lived alone in a small cottage. It was located in the front of a very deep property which stretched several hundred feet into the woods near the lake shore.

Pam rang the bell, and Mrs. Elder opened the door. "Oh, come on in, girls," she said, and showed them to a green velvet sofa in the living room.

Then she opened the top of a secretary desk across the room. "Here's the doll I was telling you about," she said, and pulled out the most beautifully dressed doll the Hollister girls had ever seen. The face was made of porcelain, delicately painted, and

"Here's the doll I told you about."

blond hair was piled high on the doll's head in the most aristocratic manner. Her gown was of yellow silk, and her petticoats were hemmed in lace.

After Holly had counted the petticoats for the third time and had untied and tied the shiny black leather shoes, the two girls rose to leave.

"Thank you so much, Mrs. Elder," Pam said.

"You're welcome." The woman smiled. "And listen, be on the lookout for prowlers!"

"Prowlers?" Pam cocked her head. "But it's still light out."

"Well, a dozen eggs disappeared from my porch yesterday in broad daylight!" the woman said.

Pam and Holly exchanged glances. *Another back-stoop thief!*

"The milkman left them," Mrs. Elder continued, "but all I found was the box and a few broken eggshells."

"We'll be careful," Holly promised. "And thanks again, Mrs. Elder."

The two girls left the house and walked along the edge of the street, which in this section had no sidewalks. Pam glanced up as they passed Mrs. Elder's back yard, and her eyes focused on the line of trees behind the property. She stopped short. "Holly, look—back there!"

"A man!" her sister gasped.

Both girls could see a face peering from behind a tree at the edge of the woods.

"Holly, I'm sure he's the one Pete and I saw in the State Park!"

"Maybe *he* took the eggs," Holly said. "Oh, I hope he doesn't chase us!"

The girls hastened along, half skipping, half running, until they felt safe once more in their own neighborhood.

"I was hoping you'd come soon," Mrs. Hollister greeted them as they entered the house, and explained that Mrs. Kane had phoned, inviting her and the girls to come to the toy library and have tea. "I said we would be there in a little while," Mrs. Hollister said. "Come, girls, Daddy left the car for us."

Pam and Holly, along with Sue, climbed in, and their mother drove across town to Washington School.

Pam showed her mother the way into the building, where Mrs. Kane met them at the door of the library.

"Hello, Mrs. Hollister," Mrs. Kane said. "Welcome to our new project."

Two other ladies were helping, placing various toys on the shelves and writing out cards for them. In the middle of the table was a pot of tea, cups and saucers, and slices of cake.

When Mrs. Kane saw the Viennese doll, she

raised her hands and exclaimed, "Oh, how beautiful! This isn't for our toy library, is it?"

Holly smiled. "Yes, it is."

When the woman heard who the donor was, she said, "I'll write Mrs. Elder a note and thank her; she is such a thoughtful woman. We'll lend this lovely doll only to girls who have already proved that they can be careful with toys."

Sue pointed to a lower shelf on which sat a walking doll. "Can I play with that, Mommy?"

"Oh, Susie! The library isn't even open yet."

Mrs. Kane laughed. "That's all right. It'll keep her occupied while we have our tea."

She wound up the doll and gave it to the little girl. Sue put it on the floor, and the doll started to walk.

"Look, Mommy, it's walking right out of the room!" Sue sang out, clapping her hands in delight.

The doll smiled proudly and walked through the door into the hall.

"Hey, come back here!" cried Sue, and ran outside. But at the door she bumped into a big boy.

Bang! Sue was thrown back and sat hard on the floor.

CHAPTER 9

Dangerous Mission

AT FIRST Sue was too startled to cry. But after her mother picked her up from the floor, she let out a wailing that filled the room. Tears gushed down her cheeks.

"I think she's more frightened than hurt," said Mrs. Kane. She looked at the boy standing outside the doorway. "You should be more careful," she scolded him.

"Joey Brill!" exclaimed Pam. "What are you doing here?"

"I wanted to see the library," Joey replied.

"Well, you didn't have to run all over Sue," Pam said, as the women looked on in surprise at the rudeness of the big boy.

"I didn't see her."

"Did you bring a toy for the new library?" Holly wanted to know.

Joey shook his head and took one step into the room. "No, I want to borrow one. You have any flying saucers?"

78

"I'm sorry. The library is not open yet," Mrs. Kane explained kindly.

Joey did not know what to say. His face grew red, and his mouth turned down at the corners. Without another word he turned and ran out of the building.

"So that's the boy who saw the flying saucer," Mrs. Kane said. "Well, I'm not convinced."

After the three Hollister girls had each eaten a piece of cake, Pam and Holly skipped out to the playground. As they went to join some girls playing in a sandbox, Alex, Pete, and Dave Mead rode in. Dave was twelve, tall, and had straight hair.

"Hi, Dave!" Pam waved. "All over your cold?"

"You bet. It's boring to stay home."

"We have some excitement coming up," Pete announced, as he stopped to talk to his sister. "Mr. Baker sent me a letter!" He pulled an envelope from his shirt pocket and handed it to Pam. The letter read:

Dear Pete, I wonder if the boys from the detective club would search around Lookout Mountain north of the Great Meadow. Your friend, Ed Baker.

Pam read the short note several times before saying, "That's sort of mysterious, Pete. It might be dangerous, too."

"I thought we bigger fellows could go," Pete said. "Dave and Alex and I. Right after church tomorrow."

Lookout Mountain rose abruptly at the north end of the valley. Climbers sometimes used ropes to scale the steep cliffs. Pete remembered that there were two boulder-strewn trails that led to the top, but these were located several miles around the foot of the hill, and in summer they were nearly choked with weeds and bushes.

"Good luck," Pam said. "Are you going to ask Mother?"

"Right now," her brother replied.

"Me, too," said Alex.

The three boys parked their bikes and went into the library, eager to tell of their proposed adventure.

At first Mrs. Hollister was skeptical. "I don't know what to think about Mr. Baker," she said. "If he's looking for the monster, why doesn't he make the search himself?"

"I think I know the reason," Pete replied. "It might be too obvious."

"That's right," Alex said. "If we go, it looks like we're just on an all-day hike."

"What about you, Dave?" Mrs. Hollister asked.

"I can go."

"Well, I don't know about Alex," Mrs. Kane put in. "I think it's too dangerous."

"Jeepers, Mom," Alex pleaded. "Dad does dangerous things all the time, and he doesn't get hurt."

"I realize that you're all brave boys," Mrs. Kane went on. She hesitated a moment and added, "You know, Alex, we're supposed to visit Uncle Arthur tomorrow."

"You can go without me. He won't mind."

"And you'll have to edge the garden, and—"

"I'll do it right now; my other Saturday jobs, too. Please, Mother!"

"Well, all right." Mrs. Kane gave her permission with a pleading glance at Mrs. Hollister. "But you must all promise to be very careful!"

"We will!" the boys said in unison. Then they hastened out and jumped on their bikes.

"We'll help you, Alex," Pete volunteered.

Alex said that besides the garden work, the front and back stairs had to be swept and the kitchen floor mopped.

The three boys worked together and had the chores finished in a couple of hours. It was agreed that they would meet at Pete's home that evening to plan their hike.

Shortly after supper the friends met in the Hollisters' basement. They decided that each would carry a pack with lunch and a canteen of water.

"We'd better bring some ropes, too," Pete said, "to help us climb those steep cliffs."

The door opened upstairs, and Pam called down, "Don't forget the walkie-talkies!"

"Good idea."

Pete went to a closet and took out three sets belonging to the Hollister children.

"This way we can separate but still keep in touch," he explained.

Sunday after church the boys set out with knapsacks on their backs and walkie-talkies slung over their shoulders. An hour later they parked their bicycles and continued on foot, climbing the gentle slope of the valley toward Lookout Mountain, which glistened in the sun.

It was decided not to separate until they had reached the top of the cliffs. Pete and Alex scrambled on ahead, with Dave following. When they came to the base of a stony slope, Alex worked his way up first, grabbing onto bushes and jutting rocks. Then he tied one end of his rope to a tree and flung the other down the cliff.

Dave caught it first and began to pull himself up. Pete followed. Soon the two came to the lip of the cliff, where Alex reached out a helping hand.

"Phew! I'm bushed!" Dave said. They sat down to rest for a few minutes. After taking several swigs of water from their canteens, the hikers continued upward. The way was steep and rocky until they came to the crest of the hill.

It was a flat plateau about a quarter of a mile wide before dropping off into a valley on the other side.

Keeping one another in sight, the companions pushed through the heavy woods. The sun beat on their backs, and their shirts grew damp.

"Hey, Pete, let's take a break," Dave said after another hour. The boys threw off their knapsacks and sat down at the base of a huge rock, mopping their faces.

"Those packs get heavier by the minute." Alex grinned and shook droplets from his forehead.

"When we eat our lunch, they'll be lighter," Dave quipped.

"I could chow down right now," Pete said but added quickly, "We'd better search some more first."

The boys stood up. This time they would walk several hundred yards apart, keeping in touch with their walkie-talkies.

"Let's go slow now," Pete suggested. He stayed in the middle. Alex walked out of sight to the left and Dave to the right.

Pete held the mike to his face. "Alex, Dave, do you read me?"

"Loud and clear."

"Okay. Forward. But not too fast. Look for anything that might be a clue."

Pete pushed on ahead. The only sounds were twigs breaking under his feet, the scurrying of a squirrel, or the chirping of a few birds high in the trees.

Suddenly Alex said, "Hey, Pete, someone has been up here recently. I just found a whittled stick."

"Nice going, Alex. Put it in your sack. Anything on your side, Dave?"

"Guys! I found something!"

"Negative."

The boys kept plodding ahead. Pete saw nothing unusual, but all at once Dave's voice came excitedly over the walkie-talkie.

"Guys, I've found something!"

"What?" asked Pete.

Dave reported a small cave entrance in the side of a rocky wall.

"It's blocked by iron bars," Dave said. "You know, just like in a prison."

Pete and Alex both listened excitedly, then Pete said, "Alex, come this way. We'll go see Dave's discovery."

But before Alex could reply, Dave's voice sounded again in a sudden cry of fright!

CHAPTER 10

A Hidden Spy

IN A FEW moments Alex came crashing through the woodland, and together the two friends raced to the spot where Dave had radioed his cry of fright.

Suddenly they heard him coming. Dave appeared through a grove of pine trees, stumbling over a protruding root, and fell to the spongy earth. He picked himself up, his face white with fear.

"What happened, did a bear chase you?" asked Alex.

"No," Dave said, after catching his breath. "It was spookier than that." He described the cave with the bars and added, "As I looked inside and radioed you, the bars began to sink into the ground! Boy, oh, boy, that scared me. I thought something was going to jump out, so I turned and ran!"

"Crickets!" Pete said. "We'd better investigate that!"

At the suggestion of Alex, the boys dropped their packs at the foot of a tall oak tree, then followed

Dave quickly to the place where he had found the cave.

"There—there it is!" Dave said, pointing to a hummock of rock and earth.

They saw a dark hole, leading into the side of the hill, but the barrier of iron bars were firmly in place.

Dave's jaw dropped. He looked in amazement from one boy to the other.

Alex rolled his eyes. "I thought you said those bars went into the ground!"

"They—they did!"

Pete went forward and grasped the bars. He tugged and tried to shake them. "They're probably set in concrete," he observed.

"You feeling all right, Dave?" Alex asked with a half-smile.

"Sure I am. I swear I saw these bars go down."

"It might have been an optical illusion, Dave," Pete suggested. "Something like mirages, that people see in the desert."

Dave gave a little halfhearted grin and said, "Maybe the heat was getting too much for me!"

The companions laughed, and all three peered through the iron bars. Inside the cave all was blackness. Pete and Alex turned after a while, but Dave continued to look. Suddenly he cried, "I see two eyes!"

His friends wheeled about. Shaking their foreheads, they strained to look into the dark interior. *Nothing!*

"But I tell you, I saw two eyes!" Dave persisted. Alex shrugged. "It *is* kind of spooky."

"You don't believe me, do you," Dave said in a hurt tone of voice.

"Sure we do," said Pete. "Hey, maybe we're all too hungry. Let's go back to those packs and have some chow."

Still keeping their eyes peeled for any possible clues, the three searchers retraced their steps to the big oak tree.

They looked for their packs and let out a cry of alarm. *The knapsacks were missing!*

"Wow!" Alex stood stock-still. Only his head moved, and his eyes scanned the deep woods which lay silently about them.

Pete pivoted, ran a few paces, stopped and listened. Nobody was in sight, and there was not a sound.

"Listen, fellows," Dave said, acting as bravely as possible. "Let's not panic. There must be an answer to this."

"Sure there's an answer," Alex replied. "Somebody stole our packs."

"Let's see if we can track the thief," Pete said. He bent down low, examining the ground at the base of the tree. Their own footprints had disturbed

The knapsacks were missing!

the soft earth, but otherwise they could find no tell-tale prints.

"Perhaps it was a big bird," said Pete, trying to break the tension with a joke.

"That big bird is spying on us right now," Alex declared. "I feel it in my bones!"

"Maybe now you'll believe my story about that goofy cave," Dave put in. "I tell you, fellows, there's something pretty kooky going on around here."

The three companions scouted the area for a few minutes but saw nothing. Pete then suggested that they hurry back to Shoreham as quickly as possible.

Their climbing ropes, still hitched to their belts, provided the boys an easy way down the cliff. Pete was the last to hit bottom. "I hope our bikes are still there," he said worriedly.

They raced to the hiding place. Much to their relief, the bicycles were exactly as they had left them. The boys hopped on and pedaled out of the State Park to the main highway.

The sun was already low in the sky when they reached Shoreham.

"My folks aren't home," said Pete, "but I guess we'll find some chow in the refrigerator."

"Let's go to my place," Dave suggested. "It's closer, anyhow."

They parked their bikes in back of Dave's house and entered the kitchen door.

"Hello, boys," Mr. Mead said, walking from the

living room with the Sunday paper in his hand. "You're back early. I thought you'd be out scouring the woods till all hours of the night."

"Creepers, Dad, wait till you hear what happened to us!" Dave said.

"Nothing bad, I hope," put in Dave's mother, as she moved beside her husband.

"Well, not *that* bad," Dave said. "We'll tell you all about it, but first can we have some eats? We're starved!"

"Go wash your hands while I make hamburgers," Mrs. Mead replied.

Later, between bites, the companions poured out the story of their strange adventure. "What's your opinion of the whole thing, Mr. Mead?" asked Pete.

"Somebody is up there in those woods!"

"You can say that again," Alex chimed in. "And listen, Mr. Mead, there's something fishy about that cave!"

"Right," Pete agreed. "It might be the key to the whole mystery. You know anything about it?"

Mr. Mead drained the last swallow from his cup of tea and put it down thoughtfully. "No, I don't remember anything about a cave," he said. "I've heard about an old revolutionary iron mine around that area, though."

"That could be it!" Dave declared.

His father nodded. "I know somebody who might tell you about it."

"Who, Mr. Mead?" Alex asked.

"Mr. Messina. He's an old fellow now, but when he was young, he worked as a surveyor when they were laying out that park area."

Dave's father told the boys that Mr. Messina lived in a small apartment over a garage in the rear of a large estate on Serpentine Road.

"Thanks, Dad!" said Dave. "We'll go see him right away."

"Well, it's almost suppertime," Mrs. Mead put in, "and besides, if you'll excuse my saying so, you all look a little beat up."

The boys glanced at their dusty clothes and smudged faces and had to laugh in spite of themselves.

"I could use a bath," Alex said sheepishly.

Pete glanced at his wrist watch. "I guess my folks are back by now," he said. "Suppose we all meet at my house in about an hour?"

His companions agreed and separated. Pete rode directly home, took a cooling shower, and told Pam about the mysterious happening on Lookout Mountain.

"Maybe you found the wrong oak tree," Pam said. "You know, it's easy to get lost in those woods."

"That did occur to me," Pete agreed, "but I'm sure we had the right one."

"But why would somebody want to steal three

knapsacks?" asked Ricky, who had listened wide-eyed to the conversation.

"Well," said Pam, "if somebody is hiding out in the woods, maybe he was hungry and wanted your lunches!"

"He could have taken the food and left the packs," Pete argued.

Finally Dave and Alex arrived. Both boys said they had tried to figure out the mystery but no luck.

"Well, let's go see if Mr. Messina can help us," said Pete.

"Don't stay too long," Mrs. Hollister warned. "It'll be dark soon."

Serpentine Road was well known to the Hollisters. It was there in a strange old house that Mrs. Neeley lived. The children had once solved a mystery for her.

"There's the old haunted house," said Pete, smiling, as they pedaled past the place.

Finally they reached the estate and rolled up a gravelly drive to a large old carriage house and garage. It nestled far behind the main house at the edge of a tree nursery. The saplings, in neat rows, were about ten feet high and in full leaf.

Pete climbed the stairs to an apartment over the garage and rang the bell. It was answered by an elderly man, gray-haired and stooped. His face, craggy and weather-beaten, was hyphenated by two bushy eyebrows. They raised when he saw the three boys.

"Evening," he said in surprise.

After Pete had made the introductions, Mr. Messina invited them inside. "Close the screen door," he said to Dave. "We do get a few mosquitoes around here."

Pete Hollister came quickly to the point. He told what had happened on Lookout Mountain. When he came to the part about the cave, Mr. Messina smiled and stroked his square jaw.

"Yes, there is a cave there," he said. "It leads to an old mine shaft. The place was considered dangerous, so the government closed the entrance with iron bars."

He glanced at Dave. "You saw the bars move?"

"They did, Mr. Messina. I'm sure of that."

"You kids are full of jokes," the old man said. "Those bars were set in concrete—to keep young fry like you from falling down the mine shaft and getting hurt."

"Would it be possible," asked Pete, "for somebody to hide in the mine shaft?"

Mr. Messina chuckled. "If he was thin as a dime and could squeeze through those bars, I guess so."

"Maybe it was an animal whose eyes I saw," said Dave.

Mr. Messina reached over to pat the boy on the shoulder. "Everybody's seeing things in Shoreham these days," he said. "They got the *monster fever*, that's what I call it."

"We're going to find out who the monster is," Pete said with determination.

"Good luck to you," the old surveyor said.

The three young detectives thanked Mr. Messina, and Pete opened the screen door to go. But before he had taken one step, he halted.

Off in a little grove of trees, he heard a voice calling, "Pongo! Pongo!"

Pete held up his hand for silence. Again the words drifted through the evening air, "Pongo! Pongo!"

CHAPTER 11

The Phantom Door

"Who's Pongo?" Dave asked.

"I don't know," Pete replied. He turned to Mr. Messina. "Somebody's on your property. He's calling a kooky name."

Mr. Messina cocked his head. "You're sure now. It's getting dark; maybe you're imagining the monster."

"Honest!" exclaimed Alex. "Somebody was calling Pongo."

"Well, now," the man went on, "this is a private estate, and no trespassers or bongos are allowed."

Pete smiled at Mr. Messina's mistake but said nothing. The old fellow explained that he was in charge of the estate while the owners had gone away for a vacation.

"I don't want any strangers wandering around here," he said, and went for a flashlight lying on a table beside the door.

Motioning the youngsters aside, Mr. Messina descended the stairs and led the way into the grove of trees. With the light flickering between the slender saplings, the old surveyor made his way to the rear of the property, which was bordered by an iron-spiked fence. Beyond this lay a heavy woods.

Pete reasoned that someone could have climbed the fence, although it would be very difficult. He borrowed the flashlight to study the soft ground beneath it.

Finally he came to what he was looking for. "See here, Mr. Messina! Somebody did climb over." Pete pointed to two deep footprints, which showed that someone had dropped down onto the grounds from the other side.

"Are there any good places to hide out on the estate?" asked Alex.

Mr. Messina looked worried. "Sure. Several buildings—the old woodshed, an old-time smokehouse, the mansion itself, and the garage behind it."

Pete went on to study the earth near the fence. He could find no indication that anyone had tried to climb back over the spiked barrier.

"It's getting too dark to search now," Pete finally said. "May we come back tomorrow, Mr. Messina?"

The man took the flashlight and walked toward his apartment without answering.

"We won't disturb anything in our search, really we won't!" Pete urged.

"But if anything should happen to you—" the man said reluctantly.

"Don't worry about us," Dave said. "We'll be very careful."

"Well, all right."

As the boys rode home again, they discussed the stranger and the odd name Pongo.

Dave thought that perhaps the monster really might be a man in disguise. "Maybe he escaped from a nuthouse or something and is just trying to frighten people."

"That estate would be a great place to hide out," said Alex. "The owner's away, and I don't think Mr. Messina can hear too well."

Next day after school, the boys met in the playground. Nearby, Pam and Ann Hunter were turning double dutch. Their friends skipped in and out of the two looping ropes as they slapped against the pavement with a steady tempo.

"Are you going to Mr. Messina's place now?" asked Pam.

"Yes," Pete replied. He stood astride his bicycle with his school books in the carrier basket.

"I'd like to come, too," said Pam.

Just then Ricky and Holly dashed in between the turning ropes. Ricky waved his arms like a flying duck each time he leaped into the air. Then the two youngsters slid out between the ropes and raced over to their older brother.

"We want to go, too," the redhead called out.

Dave and Pete were doubtful about this. "It's a

private estate," Pete said. "Mr. Messina agreed we could come back, but he didn't mention anybody else."

"Pam's going!" Holly protested.

"Well, she's big," replied Pete.

"But we want to catch the monster," said Ricky, wrinkling his nose and squinting up at his brother.

"I have an idea," Pam put in as she stopped turning. She handed her end of the rope to Ricky. "Here, why don't you two skip rope for a while. We'll go and investigate and then tell you all about it, promise!"

Ann Hunter gave her end to Holly, adding, "There's a hopscotch game, too." She pointed to a place where two little girls Holly's age were playing off to one side of the yard.

Leaving the two younger Hollisters to enjoy themselves, Pam joined the boys. They set off speedily toward Serpentine Road, stopping briefly to get their walkie-talkies.

Mr. Messina was trimming a hedge when they arrived.

"Here we are," said Pete, hopping off his bicycle. "And we brought my sister Pam."

"All of us are members of the detective club," Dave spoke up.

Pete explained that they would fan out over the large estate and keep in touch with each other with their walkie-talkies.

"Good idea," Mr. Messina said, continuing to snip at the hedge. "Look around all you want, but don't disturb anything. I haven't heard any bongos all night, and I'm sure whoever it was got away."

In the daylight things looked quite different to the young sleuths. Besides the main house, which was made of stone and constructed in a large L-shape, there were four other buildings. These included the modern three-car garage, over which Mr. Messina lived, a smokehouse, an open woodshed, and a funny little round screened-in building with a roof like a Chinese hat.

"What do you call that?" asked Alex as they walked slowly around the grounds.

Pam said it was a gazebo, or summer house. "People sit out there in the evening, and the screens keep out the mosquitoes."

Now the friends began their search in earnest. They scanned the grounds, especially around the buildings.

"Look!" Pam said suddenly, bending down near the gazebo. There were footprints in the soft ground, all around the place!

"Whoever it was," said Pete, down on his hands and knees, "he stood on his toes." The boy pointed out two deep impressions.

"Probably to look at something on the roof, I would guess," Dave said.

Pam and Alex stepped back to look at the sloping

roof, but there was no evidence that anyone had climbed up on it.

"Okay," Pete said after a while. "Dave and I will go look at the fence again." They left through the grove of trees.

Pam walked toward the garage, while Alex carefully circled the stone house. He looked for signs of an intruder but could find nothing. Whoever was looking for Pongo had not tried to enter the house.

Alex spoke into his radio. "The house seems to be clear, Pete."

Pete acknowledged the report and replied that he and Dave were still looking. The two boys walked the entire length of the fence. Near one side of the property, where the woods were the thickest, Dave pointed to a spike. "Hey, Pete, what's hanging on there?"

Pete glanced up. "Looks like a thread. It may be a clue. Here, let me boost you up, Dave."

Making a stirrup of his two hands, he lifted Dave until his friend's hand reached the spike. Dave pulled off the thread and dropped to the ground.

"Seems as if somebody snagged his clothes."

"Probably while he was trying to get away last night," Pete said.

The thread, about four inches long, had come from brown material.

"Let's take it back and show Pam," Dave suggested. He spoke into his walkie-talkie, "Are you there, Pam?"

"I'm here, Dave."

"I found a clue. We'll bring it right over to show you."

"All right, I'll wait here—oh, dear!" exclaimed Pam.

"What's the matter?" Pete asked.

"The garage door opened. There must be someone inside!"

Without waiting to reply, the two boys raced through the grove of trees to the garage. When they arrived at Pam's side, Alex was running up from the house. They looked at the gaping garage entrance. One car was inside, but nobody was to be seen.

"Did anyone come out?" Pete asked his sister.

"No! It's like—like a phantom opened the door!" Pam said, still a little scared.

Hurried footsteps on the driveway caused the youngsters to turn around. Mr. Messina came waddling toward them, a pained expression on his face.

"I told you not to fool around the property!" he said. "Why did you open that door?"

"We didn't!" Pam said. "It opened up by itself."

"Do you expect me to believe that?" the man replied, red-faced.

"Somebody must be inside," said Alex. "Let's look."

"Why did you open that door?"

Mr. Messina held up a hand. "No. You stay here. I'll go."

He went in and switched on the light. They watched him look about the garage, but there was hardly a place to hide, except in the car. The old fellow opened all four doors and even examined the trunk. Then he went over to press a button next to a side door. The large overhead door of the garage shut again, and Mr. Messina stepped out from the side entrance.

"I don't know why you had to tell a fib," he said, looking squarely at Pam.

"But—but Mr. Messina," Pam started to say; he interrupted her, however.

"All right, that's all the searching you're going to do around this property!"

The children walked dejectedly down the driveway. Before reaching the road, Pete turned back to the old surveyor. He told him what they had found on the rear fence and added, "If you do find anybody on the estate, would you please tell Officer Cal Newberry of the Shoreham police?"

Mr. Messina grumbled that he would, then returned to clipping the hedge.

Before mounting their bicycles, Pete showed Pam the clue. The girl rubbed it between her fingers. "It's wool," she said, "from somebody's trousers, I would say."

All four children rode on in silence for a few

minutes, sad to think that Mr. Messina thought they were telling a lie.

"There must have been somebody in that garage. I just can't understand it!" Pam sighed.

Dave Mead stopped off at his home, and when the remaining trio came to the Hollister house, Alex waved good-by and continued on.

Pete and Pam parked their bikes in the garage, took their schoolbooks, and walked to the front door. Their mother was just putting the telephone down, and she turned to them with an unhappy look.

"Is anything wrong, Mother?" Pam asked.

"Mrs. Kane just called. That beautiful Viennese doll that you and Holly got—it's missing from the toy library!"

CHAPTER 12

A Clue in School

"Oh, how terrible!" said Pam. "Do you suppose someone could have borrowed the doll ahead of time?"

Mrs. Hollister shook her head. "No, Mrs. Kane thinks it was stolen. The toy library doesn't open until tomorrow."

Their mother went on to say that the Hollisters had been invited to a short ceremony in the auditorium the next day, at which time the principal of the Washington School would dedicate the new toy library.

"Crickets! And that was the best toy they had," said Pete, "—for girls, that is."

At supper that evening all the children, along with their parents, talked about the strange happenings of the day. They made more than a hundred guesses about the spooky garage door and the mysterious disappearance of the Viennese doll but could not solve the riddles.

Suddenly someone knocked on the front door.

Sue squirmed from her chair and ran to greet their caller.

"Mommy, Daddy, it's Officer Cal!" she cried out.

"Oh, please come in," Mrs. Hollister said, "and join us for dessert."

The policeman strode in, carrying little Sue in his arms. "I can't stay long, but I would like to ask you something about the toy library."

"Were you there?" Pete asked.

"Yes, just now, and frankly I'm baffled."

Officer Cal said he would have a piece of Mrs. Hollister's upside-down cake, and the children's father pulled up an extra chair to the table.

As his wife spooned some whipped cream on the cake for the policeman, Officer Cal went on: "There was no sign of a forced entry into the building. It would take a cat burglar to get inside and steal that doll."

"Maybe it was an inside job," Ricky said, wiping his mouth with a napkin and looking very wise.

Sue, who sat on a cushion so that her chin could reach the top of the table, licked some whipped cream off her spoon and said, "I didn't know that cats were burglars."

Before the policeman could explain that a cat burglar was one who prowled around and entered by upstairs windows, Sue cocked her head. "White

Nose isn't a cat burglar, and I know her kittens will never go wrong."

Everyone laughed. Mrs. Hollister assured her little girl that White Nose was an honest kitty and that her babies would always be honest like their mother.

When dessert was finished, Officer Cal quietly beckoned to Pete and Pam. He also asked their parents to join him in the living room, while Ricky, Holly, and Sue dashed out the back door to play.

"I'd like to get your opinion," Officer Cal began, "about Joey Brill."

"You mean in regard to the doll theft?" asked Pam.

"Yes. Joey had come to the library and been denied a toy. Perhaps he took the doll to be mean."

"I don't think so," said Pam. "He would have taken something that boys like."

Pete spoke up. "Officer Cal, I don't think that Joey would break into the school."

His parents were quick to agree. They said that Joey was sly and played tricks, but they felt that he would not do anything really dishonest.

Officer Cal mused for a minute. "Well, the only possible way to get into the building, without jimmying a door, is through a skylight in the gymnasium on the top floor. But it would take a mountain climber or a very daring boy to get in there."

"In that case," Mr. Hollister said, "perhaps Ricky is right about an inside job."

"We'll solve it somehow," Officer Cal said. He thanked the Hollisters for their hospitality, and as he was about to leave, Pete said, "Did you find any more clues about the monster?"

"No. How about the detective club?"

Pete told of the mysterious voice calling "Pongo," and Pam related the strange opening of the garage doors.

The officer thought that perhaps someone had a dog named Pongo and had been looking for him. As for the garage door, he said that sometimes the electronic works went out of order.

"I hope Mr. Messina knows that," said Pam.

Officer Cal smiled. "I'm keeping an eye on that place while the owners are away. Next time I stop by, I'll tell Mr. Messina that you're good kids."

"Thanks," said Pam, and waved good-by.

The story of the missing Viennese doll spread quickly through the neighborhood, and the next day in school the Hollisters thought so much about the mystery that they could hardly keep their minds on their work.

The toy library was to be opened that afternoon, so Mrs. Hollister had asked her children to hurry home so they could all go to Washington School for the ceremony.

Classes over, Ricky and Holly were joined by Jeff and Ann Hunter.

"Do you suppose that Joey Brill or Will Wilson took the Viennese doll?" asked Ann.

Holly was doubtful about this, but Ricky felt that the two bullies were involved.

They had walked only a block when Will and Joey passed on their bicycles.

"Why don't you give the doll back, Joey?" Ricky called out.

Instead of ignoring the younger children, the boys wheeled about, slid off the bicycle seats, and faced the smaller ones.

"We didn't take any old doll," Joey exclaimed.

"Of course not, and don't say we did!" stormed Will Wilson.

The big boys shuffled closer, and Holly said, "Don't you hurt us!"

In answer Joey leaned forward and tugged one of her pigtails.

"Ouch!" she cried.

The two bullies laughed, hopped on their bicycles, and pedaled off.

Ricky frowned. "I want to see where they are going!"

"But Mother told us to come right home," Holly objected.

"Well, it won't take long," Ricky said. "Don't forget, we're all members of the detective club, and it's up to us to find that doll!"

After talking it over, the children decided to follow Joey and Will as far as they could. They were still in sight, riding slowly and occasionally making figure-eight patterns. Finally they disappeared.

Ricky hastened after them, with the others following. Taking care to conceal themselves behind trees and bushes along the way, they trailed Joey and Will right to the lake shore. There the bullies rested their bicycles against a tree and sauntered along the pebbly waterfront.

Like small kittens following two big cats, Ricky, Holly, Jeff, and Ann crouched down behind a low stone wall which bordered the back of a property, and cautiously peered over the top.

"Ha, ha, here it is!" Joey said. He bent down to pick up something from near the water's edge.

"Make it go again," Will called out. The big boy whirled about, and something flew from his hand. It landed with a bang, half in and half out of the water.

"What was that?" Jeff whispered.

"I didn't get a good look," Ricky replied.

Joey and Will walked along farther and picked up the object. Just then Will turned about, and the four had to duck out of sight.

"That's a beauty; there it goes!" Will shouted.

Again a bang was heard far along the beach.

"Oh, I wish I could see what they are doing!" said Holly. She was interrupted by a faint call in the

"What was that?" Jeff whispered.

distance, and the Hollisters immediately recognized Pam's voice.

"Oh, she's calling us!" Ricky said. "We have to go with Mother!"

The four children sneaked back to find Pam.

"Come on, you're late," Pam scolded. "You weren't supposed to play on the way home."

Holly explained that they had been trailing Joey and Will.

"Forget about them now," Pam said.

Ricky and Holly said good-by to Jeff and Ann. Then, with Pam holding her bicycle steady, Holly climbed in the basket, while Ricky straddled the back fender. Pam set off with her heavy load, careful to stay far to one side of the street.

When they arrived home, Mrs. Hollister was waiting with Pete and Sue.

"Hurry up," she said smiling, "or we'll be late for the grand opening."

In no time at all they were on their way, and soon the car was parked in front of Washington School. The Hollisters hurried inside. The front door led directly through a hall into a large auditorium, where about a hundred people had gathered. The principal was about to speak. After the Hollisters were seated and a few other latecomers arrived, the ceremony began.

First the principal told of the need for such a toy library. "There's another one in the city of

Baltimore," he said, "and it's a great success. We hope the Washington School toy library also will succeed."

He thanked individuals for bringing so many toys to the school, and also expressed regret that the Viennese doll had been taken.

After his short speech, the principal invited everyone to see the new library.

Sue and Holly trailed behind the others as they walked from the auditorium.

"We've already seen it," Sue declared. "Let's look at the school, Holly."

Her tomboy sister thought this would be a good idea. Tickling her nose with a pigtail, she took Sue's hand, turned down an empty corridor, and walked along on tiptoes so as not to be heard.

The classrooms were empty, and all was still and quiet. Holly sniffed the nice smell of old wood, new books, and little children. They were about to turn another corner, when a whispering sound came from the corridor.

The girls stood still and listened. Suddenly a man turned the corner. He jumped when he noticed the startled girls but hastened past them as if they were not there. Soon he was out of sight.

"He acted funny, didn't he," Sue said, baffled.

"Maybe he went into the library," Holly replied. "Come on, let's find out."

They followed the man. When they reached the

library door, they saw him inside. Holly beckoned to Pam. "See that man over there? He was whispering in the hall."

Pam looked about until her eyes found the one to whom her sister was pointing.

"Yes, I see him. What did he say?"

"Pongo, Pongo."

The words made Pam shiver a bit. What did this man have to do with the monster mystery, and who was Pongo? She decided to confront him directly.

"Are you looking for Pongo?" she asked the stranger, as he gazed over the shelves laden with toys.

The man turned around. He was short, about her father's age, and had small piercing eyes and black brows. "I beg your pardon," he said. "Are you talking to me?"

"Yes," Pam said, and repeated her question.

"I don't know what you are talking about," he replied indignantly.

"Oh, yes, you do," Holly chirped. "We saw you out in the hall!"

"It must have been somebody else!" With that he turned, slid behind a group of people, and headed for the door. Before Pam had a chance to tell her mother, he had vanished.

By five-thirty the last of the visitors had left the school. It was locked for the evening. On their way home in the station wagon, Pam told about the stranger that Sue and Holly had seen. Before they had reached home, Ricky bragged about how they had trailed Joey and Will.

"What were they playing with?" asked Pete.

"We didn't exactly see."

Pete looked at his sister and whispered something in her ear. When the car stopped in the Hollisters' driveway, Pam said, "Mother, may Pete and I go off for about an hour before supper?"

"Yes," Mrs. Hollister replied.

The two older children ran back to the lake front and walked carefully along the shore toward the spot where Will and Joey had been seen playing. No one was in sight except a few fishermen, drifting in their boats offshore.

"This might be the answer to Joey's fantastic story," Pete said. "Crickets, if we could only find out!"

Now they had reached the spot where the youngsters had spied out from behind the low stone wall. Pete walked near the water's edge while Pam searched the stony beach.

Finally she called out excitedly. "Pete, come here!"

He ran to her side. At Pam's feet lay an old, battered trash-can lid. Pete picked it up.

"Crickets. I'll bet this really is what we're looking for! Watch, Pam!"

Pete swung his arm in a wide arc, and the lid sailed through the air. As it ascended, the Hollisters recalled the picture in the newspaper.

"That's it, all right!" Pam cried "—the flying saucer!"

CHAPTER 13

Chocolate Nose

CERTAIN that they had discovered the answer to Joey Brill's fake picture, Pete and Pam raced home with the trash-can lid. Pam remained near the dock while Pete raced inside to get his camera. Several pictures were left on the roll.

Pete set the shutter speed for a hundredth of a second and said to Pam, "All ready. When I throw the lid into the air, take the picture at its highest point."

He gave her the camera, braced both of his feet, and swung his arm high. Up went the lid! *Snap* went the camera.

"I think that was a good picture, Pete!" said Pam. Just to make sure, she took two more shots before her mother called them in to dinner.

"Crickets, this ought to be good," Pete said.

"Let's take them to Dave's house," Pam suggested. "He has a developing and printing kit."

Pete phoned. He told Dave that as soon as they

finished their homework, they would be over with the roll of film.

"Okay," Dave said happily. "I'll start my work right away. See you later."

Pete and Pam took their books upstairs, where it was quieter, and after concentrating hard on their homework, they hastened down again before it was nine o'clock. By that time the younger children were already in bed.

It was only a short walk to Dave's house. They found him waiting in his basement darkroom, which had a special dim-colored light glowing from the ceiling.

"Oh, boy, I hope they come out," Dave said, as he unwound the roll of film and put the strip into his developing tank.

Pete and Pam looked on as Dave checked a clock on the wall of the darkroom. "That's enough time for the developer," he said, poured out the liquid, and washed the film. Then he poured on another chemical to complete the process.

"The negatives are ready," Dave announced. He examined them, with the Hollisters pressing close for a glimpse. The four pictures of the flying-saucer garbage-can cover were sharp and clear. Pam chuckled when the other pictures showed the Hollister girls in their Easter bonnets.

"Let's print up the flying-saucer pictures first," Pete said.

Dave put the strips of film in an enlarger and in no time at all produced large prints of the flying garbage-can lid. They were still damp when the trio went upstairs to show them to Dave's parents.

"I still have the newspaper picture around here somewhere," Mrs. Mead said. She found it in a desk drawer, and comparisons were made.

"That's it, all right," said Dave, chuckling. "Look Pete, your picture has the same angle and everything."

"Wait until the newspaper sees this!" said Pam.

She and her brother thanked Dave and hurried home with the evidence. They raced inside to show Mr. and Mrs. Hollister.

"So those rascals Joey and Will have been uncovered," Mr. Hollister said with a wide grin.

Pam pleaded with her mother to let both of them go to the newspaper office early next morning. "You can write us an excuse, can't you, Mother, please?" said Pam.

"Well, I think it can wait until the afternoon."

"No, Mother. We must get it in tomorrow's newspaper so people will stop worrying about creatures from outer space."

"That sounds reasonable enough to me," her father said, and Mrs. Hollister finally agreed.

"There's been so much scary business about flying saucers and monsters," she said, "I'll be glad when this whole mystery is settled."

At breakfast next morning Pete and Pam made Holly and Ricky promise not to tell anybody in school about their discovery.

"They'll see it in the newspapers soon enough," said Pete.

Mrs. Hollister wrote a note to the teachers, and the older children set off with their father, who dropped them off at the newspaper office. Pete and Pam went straight to the desk of Mr. Kent.

When the editor saw them, he said, "Good morning, children. Do you have some big scoop for me?"

"We sure have," said Pete.

Pam's hands trembled with excitement. "We caught a flying saucer!"

"Here now, what's this?" the editor asked, and Pam handed him the sheaf of pictures.

"Hmm," the newspaper man said, leaning back in his swivel chair to study the pictures. "So you saw the flying saucer, too."

"It's a flying garbage-can top," Pete said. "We found it on the beach. Joey and Will had been playing with it."

"Well, I'll be a monkey's uncle!" the editor exclaimed. He rose and went to a stack of papers on a desk near the window. There he quickly found the photo of Joey Brill's flying saucer. "They're the same, all right. No doubt of it."

"What are you going to do now?" asked Pam.

"Print a retraction," Mr. Kent replied without hesitation. With a wink at the Hollisters he added, "This story will be even better than the first one."

The editor pressed a button, and soon a reporter entered his office. "I've got a great story for you here, Jack," Mr. Kent said. "Listen carefully to what Pete and Pam have to say, and give them full credit for uncovering the phony flying saucers."

"So it was a hoax!" The young man grinned. Immediately he started to take several pages of notes, and when he had finished, he said, "I would also like to use the pictures."

"They really belong to Dave Mead," Pam said. "He developed them."

"We'll mention that in the story, too."

Once the report was finished, Pete and Pam hastened to The Trading Post, which was close by. From there Indy Roades drove them to school.

When Miss Hanson read Pete's excuse note, she smiled, and the boy took his seat.

"Can't you get up on time?" Joey Brill said in a loud whisper.

"No talking," the teacher reproached Joey, and went on with the lesson.

By the time school was out that afternoon, some of the teachers were grinning at Joey Brill and Will Wilson.

"Hey, they think we're great," Joey boasted.

But before the bullies could leave the building, several of the children had heard the news.

"Hi, you big fakes," Donna Martin said.

"What do you mean?" Will asked, giving the girl a shove.

"It's all in the papers," one of the other pupils called out. "The Hollisters found out all about your flying-saucer garbage lid!"

Joey and Will turned beet red. They hastened out of school, jumped on their bikes, and without looking right or left, pedaled quickly away.

The Hollisters wondered what the Brills and the Wilsons would say to their sons that afternoon, but whatever it was, the fibbers were not affected. They both drove past the Hollisters later, not looking a bit ashamed of what they had done.

"Hello phony," Ricky teased, making sure to keep a good distance from Joey Brill.

"Ha, ha," Joey said. "We fooled everybody, even the newspaper."

"Ricky Hollister, you must be nutty!" Will Wilson went on. "You said you saw the flying saucers, too! You're just as bad as we are!"

Ricky did not know what to say. He quietly went inside the house and talked to his mother. "I wasn't telling a lie, Mommy, really I wasn't," the boy said, and explained he *had* seen something on the lake. He confessed that he was not sure if it had landed on the water or was only floating there.

"Forget about it, Ricky," Mrs. Hollister said, putting an arm around the boy. "At least you know there aren't any flying saucers and the little green men won't be climbing in your window tonight."

Ricky was relieved and ran outside to play again.

Even Sue and Holly were glad to know that the saucer from outer space wasn't flying around Pine Lake. When both girls went to bed that night, they slept extra soundly. As a result they wakened ahead of everybody else.

Holly looked out of her window to see a heavy mist covering Pine Lake. She roused Sue gently.

"Baby, come on," she said. "I'm hungry. Let's go downstairs and have breakfast by ourselves."

Sue liked the idea of an adventure together in the early morning. Both girls put on their robes and slippers, opened the door of their bedroom quietly, and tiptoed unheard down the stairway to the kitchen.

Holly heard a meow in the basement. She opened the door, and White Nose stepped out, stretching each leg individually before walking stiffly across the kitchen floor.

"Meow," said the cat again.

"She's hungry like we are," Holly said. "Sue, would you like some chocolate milk?"

"Oh, goody," the little girl replied.

Holly pulled up a chair, climbed on it, and reached into the kitchen cabinet for the box of chocolate powder, but the box, its lid on loosely, slipped out of her fingers.

BANG.

It hit the chair, and the top flew off. All the chocolate powder spilled down on White Nose!

"Now you've done it!" said Sue. "Now our kitty isn't White Nose any more."

"What do you mean?"

"She's Chocolate Nose."

Holly quickly got a dustpan and brush and cleaned up the powder from the floor. But the cat's fur was full of the chocolate dust. Together the girls took White Nose outside to brush her.

The fog had lifted a little, and the youngsters could see the outline of their dock, damp with morning mist.

When Chocolate Nose was White Nose once more, the girls stood up. Sue carried the pet under her arm like a purse. She turned to enter the kitchen again when she stopped suddenly. "Holly, look over there!"

"A man!" Holly gasped. "And he is chasing a little boy."

Along the misty shore, a man was in hot pursuit of what looked like a small boy.

"Stop! Stop chasing him!" Holly called out.

Both figures ran past the Hollister dock in the fog. Then they were lost in the eerie white blanket.

"Now you've done it!" said Sue.

The two girls, feeling the dampness through their slippers, hastened to the edge of the lake but could see nobody.

"They ran right across our dock," Holly said.

Large prints on the moist wood had been made by the man. He had worn sneakers. The crisscross marks on the soles stood out clearly and sparkled in the sun, which shone big and red over the eastern horizon.

"But look at these other marks," said Sue. "They don't look like a boy's."

The two girls hunkered down to examine the other footprints.

"At least he didn't wear any shoes," Sue went on.

"How could he," Holly cried. "'Cause he's a monster. Look, Sue, that boy had animal toes."

"I don't believe it," said Sue. "Anyhow, I'm hungry. I want my chocolate milk."

Hand in hand the girls walked back to the kitchen. There was enough powder in the can for Holly to make two brimming cups of chocolate. Then the girls fed White Nose and took a pan of milk down into the basement for her kittens.

When this was done, they played with their dolls until the grownups came downstairs.

"Mommy," said Sue, "we saw a man chasing the monster this morning."

"You what?" Mrs. Hollister asked, nearly dropping the coffeepot.

"Yes, we did," said Holly, and her head bobbed up and down. "It was a little-boy monster with animal feet!"

CHAPTER 14

Treetop House

"You were dreaming, Holly," Ricky said, as he poured more cream on his cereal.

"Don't say that!" Holly defended herself. "You saw something funny on the lake, too, didn't you?"

"Yes, but it wasn't a little-boy monster with animal feet. That's silly!"

Pete, however, was not convinced that the story of his two small sisters was all imagination. "If only Zip had been out of the house early that morning," he thought to himself. But the collie had been lying on the rug beside his bed. Pete looked across the table at his sister Pam.

"Maybe they're right," he said in a low voice. She nodded.

When breakfast was over, Pete and Pam asked Holly and Sue to show them the footprints on the dock. But by the time they got there, the foggy dampness had evaporated under the bright sun and there were no traces left.

On the way to school, the older Hollisters discussed the mystery while Ricky and Holly scampered on ahead.

"The answer is in the woods, I'm sure of that," said Pete. "And the only way we'll solve this mystery is to keep on scouting around until we find it!"

"Maybe we could go on a picnic supper there this evening," Pam suggested.

"Who?"

"You and I and perhaps Dave and Alex."

"Leave the kids home?"

"Yes." Pam thought this would be better. They could scour a wider area. "And," she added, "you can show me where this old mine entrance is. I've never seen it."

"Good idea!"

At recess that morning, plans were laid for the picnic. Pam would supply the sandwiches, Dave Mead the cokes, and Alex dessert. It was agreed they would leave from Dave's home about four-thirty.

At a quarter to five that afternoon, bicycle wheels were humming along the road to the park. Pam's carrier basket contained neatly wrapped sandwiches, covered by a pink tablecloth. Dave carried a carton of cold drinks, while Alex had brought a white box.

"Did you get that from a bakery?" asked Pete.

"The box, yes." Alex added, "But not what's inside it."

"And what is that?" asked Pam, pedaling along beside the brown boy.

Alex grinned. "Half a homemade devil's-food cake. My mother's great at that."

"Maybe we can lure the monster with it," Pete said with a chuckle.

"Not when you taste this," Alex replied. "You'll want to eat it all yourself."

Soon they arrived at the entrance of the State Park and rode to the gate. Several cars with parents and children who also had come out for an evening picnic were parking in the lot.

The four friends pedaled past the spot where the farthest car had stopped. They pulled their bikes off the road and into the woods.

"Look, there's a good place with a table," Pam said. She pointed to a large, round stump about two feet high and spread the cloth on it. Then the food was unwrapped.

Leaning back on their elbows, the four sat on the ground. Pam passed out the sandwiches. Dave Mead snapped off the bottle tops, and the thirsty bike riders all drank deeply of the cool coke.

"This is really living!" Alex grinned.

"Enjoy it while you can," said Dave, "because we're in the home of the monster!"

"I wonder where he does really live," Alex mused, as he picked a crumb that had fallen onto his shirt front.

"Probably in a cave," said Pam.

"Or in some kind of a nest, maybe."

"Since our monster most likely is a human being," declared Pete, "I doubt that."

Now the sandwiches were finished, and Pam unwrapped the silver foil from around the devil's-food cake. The youngsters licked their lips at the sight of four huge chunks on the tree stump before them. Each helped himself, and as Pam bit into her moist piece, she said, "Umm. This is delicious."

"Here, monster, monster," Dave said, glancing about the woods. "Come get your dessert. Then we could catch you!"

But there was no reply to his coaxing except the twittering of birds and the humming of bees.

"We'd better get going," Pete said, "so we can use all the daylight possible."

Pam gathered the scraps together, put them in the tablecloth, and folded it up.

"I suggest we leave our bikes here," Dave said.

"All right," Pete agreed. "Let's go into the woods. Say, did anybody bring a compass?"

None had. Only the walkie-talkies and flashlights were on hand.

Pete looked around. "Let's stay close together," he said. "It's safer that way."

"Well, we know this place pretty well," Dave said. "I don't think we'll get lost."

Within earshot of each other, the four young

sleuths spread out and walked slowly through the woods. They stopped occasionally to look and listen.

The Hollisters knew that this area of the park bordered the meadow. Pete felt that by turning due right, they would come out in the open. Using the sun as their guide, they turned west, walked a quarter of a mile, and there it was! The grassy plain stretched broad and green, nearly a half mile wide, until it joined the woods on the opposite side again.

The youngsters walked along the edge of the forest before penetrating into the woodland once more. By now the sun had almost set.

"It'll be dark in another hour," Pete said. "I hope we come up with some clue before then."

They trudged along for a while, when suddenly they heard a flock of crows calling high in the tree-tops.

Alex stood still. "Sounds like a warning cry," he said. "Something must be disturbing the birds."

They glanced skyward to see half a dozen crows rise up from the dead branches of a gaunt oak tree. Suddenly something caught Pete's attention in a tree nearby.

"Hey! Look up there!" he said, pointing.

"Where?" Dave asked.

"That pine tree—the tallest one—near the top!"

"It's a tree house!" Alex exclaimed.

"But how did it get up there?" Dave asked, perplexed. The lower limbs of the pine did not afford climbing handholds until nearly twenty feet from the ground.

The children moved closer for a better look. Suddenly, from a high rise of ground beyond, they saw a flashing light.

"Down!" Pete hissed, and they quickly flattened themselves on the mossy earth.

"I know what it is," Dave whispered. "The sun's flashing off somebody's binoculars."

"And there—there's a man!" Pam gasped.

With hearts thumping, the young detectives watched a shadowy figure, binoculars to his eyes, walk quietly among the trees. The man was so intent upon the tree house that he did not notice anything else.

Alex advanced on knees and elbows and pressed his face close to Pete's. "He's looking at the tree house."

"Maybe he lives up there."

Alex shook his head. He did not see a ladder of any kind and doubted if anybody could scale the tree without one.

All at once the stranger put down the binoculars for a moment, and Pam could see his face. She let out a little gasp. It was the Oriental in the tan suit they had seen when they came to the woods the first time!

Peering out from the tall grass the girl looked on fascinated as the little man drew closer and closer to her. If he did not look where he was going, he might—

"Please!" Pam cried out. "Don't step on me!" She jumped up from the grass, and so did the boys.

The man's eyes bulged with surprise. He raised his hand, then suddenly turned and disappeared between two leafy trees.

"Wait!" Pete called out. "We want to talk to you!" At the same time the children followed in hot pursuit. But in vain. The stranger seemed swallowed by the earth.

Alex stopped. "He sure knows his way around," he said, disappointed.

"You said it," Pete muttered. "Well, there's no use running after him now. Let's go back and have another look at that tree house."

They trotted back to the tall pine and craned their necks, trying to peer into the nest.

"Crickets, I'd like to know whose it is," Pete said. He recalled the tree house they had once built themselves. It had not been nearly that high.

Pam looked about in the dusk and pulled Pete's arm. "It's starting to get dark," she said. "We'd better go home."

Armed with the additional clues they had found, the searchers started back to the stump where they had left their bicycles. Pete suggested they make their way to the meadow first, follow the line of the woods, then plunge back in again.

"Please! Don't step on me!"

"It won't be too hard to find. I know the way," he said confidently.

Using their flashlights now, they trotted through the woods, with Pete in the lead. He zigzagged to avoid bushes and fallen logs, and the others kept close behind him, Indian file.

Suddenly Alex called out. "Hey, Pete, look! There's the tree house again!" All four lights flashed up the trunk of the pine tree.

"He's right," Dave said. "Pete, you've taken us in a circle."

"What a dope I am," Pete scolded himself. "I should have brought my compass."

The floor of the forest was growing darker, but the afterglow in the sky above was still light enough. Now Pete walked slower and more carefully, his flashlight probing the way.

"Holy crow!" Dave said as they walked along. "If we get lost—"

"There it is!" Pete interrupted. "There's the meadow!"

The children raced out into the clearing, and Pete said, "Let's follow this line of trees now. Our bikes aren't too far away." But as he spoke, a noise sounded in the distance.

They stopped dead in their tracks. "An airplane!" Pam shouted. "Here it comes, right over the meadow!"

The running lights of an airplane became distinct

in the semidarkness. The noise of the motor stopped, and the craft descended lower and lower.

"He's probably in trouble!" Dave said.

"You're right, an emergency landing," Dave agreed. "Let's see if we can help."

Now the airplane's wheels touched down, and it rolled along the meadow toward them.

The four children, waving their flashlights, ran toward it. It was a high-winged craft with a single motor. Its white lettering was visible—N268AE.

"We can tell the pilot where he is!" Pete said, when suddenly the motor roared into life again. The plane turned around and raced across the meadow.

"He's running away from us!" Pete cried out.

CHAPTER 15

Face to Face

THE pilot gunned the engine, and the plane shot up into the air. Speechless, the four youngsters watched it lift into the sky, and followed the red and green lights until they disappeared in the black distance.

"What do you know about that!" Dave said finally.

"Crickets, he couldn't have been frightened of us!" Pete declared.

"It sure looked like he was," Alex said.

"Either that," Pam put in, "or he's trying to hide something."

"Something illegal, perhaps?" asked Alex.

"Yes," Pam answered. "Something illegal in connection with this mystery."

"Maybe he was going to meet somebody here," Dave reasoned.

"If that's the case," Pete said, "that person should be here right now."

The children turned around and looked in all directions, but the blackness of night prevented them from seeing anything farther than twenty feet away.

"Come on, we'd better get back home," Pete urged. "Mom and Dad will start worrying about us."

They followed the line of the woods for a while, then turned off into the heavy growth where their bicycles had been left. This time Pete's guess was exactly right. They took their bikes and, with flashlights bobbing, walked to the lane which led to the park entrance. Then they pedaled along, with Pam in the lead.

Suddenly she cried out in fright. A figure leaped from the roadside directly in her path! Pam swerved, dropped her light, and crashed to the ground.

The boys stopped and ran to her side. "What's the matter?" Pete cried out.

"Didn't you see it?" Pam said, still shaking. Pete looked surprised. "See what?"

"I didn't see anything either," Dave remarked, as he reached down to lift Pam's bicycle up from the ground.

The girl told them what had happened.

"What did he look like?" Pete wanted to know.

"Really I don't know," Pam replied.

"I've got the answer!" Alex said. "It must have been the person the airplane was looking for!"

"Well, whoever it was," Dave declared, "must live in the woods."

"In the tree house maybe?" Alex asked.

"Didn't you see it?" Pam said, still shaking.

Pete shrugged. "Let's get going!" he urged, and they pressed on, this time with Pete in the lead and Pam directly behind him.

"Anyone remember that plane's number?" Dave wondered when they came to the main road.

"Yes," Pam said. "N268AE."

"At least we'll be able to find out who owns it," Alex said, "and maybe solve the mystery that way."

From a distance the four young sleuths looked like a bunch of lightning bugs, flashing their lights off and on as they proceeded down the highway.

All of a sudden Pete stopped short. "Why didn't I think of that before!" he blurted out.

"Think of what?" Alex asked.

"Mr. Baker, the investigator. He wanted us to report clues to him. I think we should do it now, especially since we'll pass by his motel."

"Good idea," Pam agreed. "We can call home from there. It's getting so late."

The Lakeview Motel came into sight five minutes later, its bright neon sign announcing NO VACANCY.

They rode up to the office, parked their bikes, and went inside.

An old gentleman behind the desk looked at them over his glasses and said, "Sorry, we're all filled up."

Pete chuckled. "We don't want to stay here," he explained. "We live in Shoreham."

"I'd like to make a phone call," Pam said, and

the man pointed to a public booth on the opposite side of the entrance.

Pete gave her a dime for the call, then turned to the clerk. "We also came to see Mr. Baker. Is he in?"

The man looked at the boy curiously. "Does he know you?"

"Yes," Pete replied.

"Give me your name and I'll phone him."

While the man went to the switchboard, Pam returned from the phone booth. She had called her mother, asking her to get in touch with Mrs. Mead and Mrs. Kane. "Mother was worried," Pam reported, "but I told her everything was all right."

Just then the clerk turned back to the children. "Okay," he said. "Mr. Baker will see you. He's in room 14A."

Pete led the way along a concrete walk, past windows and doors of the motel, until he came to room 14A. He stopped to listen and heard voices inside. Then he rapped lightly on the door.

"Come in!" sounded Mr. Baker's deep voice, and Pete opened the door.

The four children trooped into the room. They stopped in surprise, however, when their eyes fell upon a man sitting in a chair next to Mr. Baker. Pam gasped and put a hand to her mouth.

It was the dark-skinned Oriental, the small man they had seen in the woods!

143

At first Pam did not know what to say. Finally she stammered, "Mr. Baker—do you know this man?"

The investigator smiled and motioned to the sofa for the children to be seated. "Yes," he replied. "He is Mr. Chandar from Borneo."

"Borneo!" Alex said. "That's part of Malaysia. We're studying it in school."

Mr. Chandar acknowledged this with a nod of his head, but he did not smile.

"Mr. Chandar is not what you might think he is," Mr. Baker went on.

"We don't know what to think," Pete declared. "We saw him in the woods again this evening."

The Malaysian said nothing but looked to the investigator for reply.

"All I can tell you is, don't worry," Mr. Baker suggested. "Mr. Chandar and I are working together on the monster mystery. By the way, do you have any new clues?"

"Crickets!" said Pete. "I'll say we do."

He then unfolded the story of the evening's activities, starting with the tree house and Mr. Chandar spying on it. When Pete reached the part about the strange airplane, the two men exchanged significant glances.

"And you got the number, Pam?" Mr. Baker asked.

Pam repeated it from memory, and both men pulled pencils from their pockets and jotted it down.

"That might lead us to something," Mr. Baker said.

"Lead us to what?" Pete asked. "Everybody is becoming impatient about this mystery, Mr. Baker. Can't you tell us what it's all about?"

"Well, you know almost as much as we do," the investigator said thoughtfully.

"Almost," Pam repeated. "But what is your secret, Mr. Baker?"

"I wish I could tell you now, but I can't. It's true, there is a secret involved."

"When will you tell us?" Pete wanted to know.

"Tomorrow evening. I'll get in touch with you then. Meanwhile, keep your eyes open."

Mr. Baker saw the children to the door. Pete turned around. "Nice to meet you, Mr. Chandar," he said. "Hope you find what you're looking for."

The Oriental bowed slightly, and the youngsters left. They mounted their bicycles and pedaled the rest of the way into Shoreham, still pondering the strange riddle of the mysterious Indonesian man.

"I wonder why Mr. Chandar is on this case," Pete said.

"I think maybe he's the monster himself!" Alex declared.

Twenty minutes later they dropped Dave off at his house, then continued on.

"So long, Alex," Pete said, as they came to the Hollisters' driveway.

"What do we do next, Pete?" Alex asked.

"Check on the airplane number. We can do that tomorrow."

"How?"

"At the airport. Meet us there after school."

"Okay. So long."

The younger children were already in bed when Pete and Pam entered their living room. Mrs. Hollister seemed quite agitated. After hearing the story about the airplane, she said, "I think this matter should be turned over to the police. It's getting too dangerous for the detective club to handle."

"Well, crickets, Mom," Pete spoke up. "I think we're pretty close to solving the case."

"At least we can find out who owns the plane," Pam said.

"Besides that," Pete urged, "Mr. Baker's going to let us in on the secret tomorrow night!"

Mrs. Hollister looked at her two children thoughtfully. "You're right. You shouldn't give up now. I'm going to help you."

"Now you're talking, Elaine," Mr. Hollister said, winking.

"Oh, Mother, I love you!" Pam flung her arms about Mrs. Hollister. "We haven't failed to solve a mystery yet."

"And you won't fail in this one either. In fact,

I'll drive you all to the airport tomorrow." Mrs. Hollister cocked her head and rolled her eyes, adding, "I'd like to know who owns that airplane myself!"

Fortunately, Pete and Pam had little homework that night. They went to bed and rose early to be sure their lessons were prepared. They went off to school next morning, eager to return and go to the airport.

When they arrived home that afternoon, their mother was ready to leave. "This will be an adventure for all of us," she said.

The five Hollisters and Dave Mead piled into the station wagon. On the way Mrs. Hollister stopped and treated them to giant-sized soft ice cream cones, which they licked contentedly until the airport came in sight.

The car was parked, and they marched inside the large building, where passengers moved to and fro from the airline counters, waiting their turns to board the departing airplanes.

Alex was already waiting for them at the counter of the largest airline. Pete asked for the person in charge. From behind the partition stepped a short man in a neat blue uniform. A small label over his left breast pocket bore the words *Mr. Pickett.* "And what can I do for you?" he asked, looking at the visitors.

Pete asked if he could find the name of an airplane's owner by the registration number.

"Of course I can," Mr. Pickett replied. "Why don't you step this way?"

Leaving the others behind, Pete and Pam entered his office, where Pam repeated the number of the mysterious airplane, "N268AE. Does that sound right to you, sir?" she asked.

The man explained that the letter N was for American registry. "This is usually followed by four numerals and another letter," he said, "but in some cases there may be three numerals and two letters. Your number sounds legitimate, all right."

He pulled a large directory from his desk and began to scan it page by page.

Finally he came to the number they had mentioned. "Here's the man you're looking for," Mr. Pickett said. "That plane is owned by the Reverend Horace Wilkie."

"A clergyman?" Pete asked, surprised.

"Yes. I've heard of him. He flies his plane all over the country."

Pete turned dejectedly toward his sister. "That sinks our case!" he mumbled.

CHAPTER 16

Hot on the Trail

"OF COURSE," said Mrs. Hollister, when she heard who owned the airplane. "Mr. Wilkie is known as the Flying Preacher. He lives on a farm not too far from here."

"I don't think it was him at all," Pete said. "What would a flying preacher be doing on the meadow in the State Park?"

Ricky suggested that they go see the man to find out for sure. "Besides," he said, "maybe he'll give us a ride in his airplane."

"Come on. Jump in," Mrs. Hollister said, and went to the car. "We'll pay Mr. Wilkie a visit." The station wagon rolled out of the parking area just as a small airplane was landing. The children craned their necks to watch it hiss over their heads and feather down on the runway.

"I love baby airplanes," said Sue. "They're so cute."

It did not take long to reach the Wilkie farm, where the name stood out boldly on a roadside mailbox. A gravel driveway, circling three old apple trees, led to the front door of the colonial farmhouse. Pam slid out of her seat and banged the brass knocker. A short, blond woman answered. Her questioning blue eyes went from Pam to the station wagon.

"Yes? May I help you?"

"Are you Mrs. Wilkie?"

"That's right."

"Is your husband in?"

"We want a ride in his airplane!" Ricky blurted.

Pam shook her head in annoyance. "It's not that, Mrs. Wilkie. We want to know the number."

"We only have one airplane."

Pam sighed and smiled. "I'm going to start over again, Mrs. Wilkie." First she introduced herself, her family, and the two boys with them.

"Oh, I know who you are," the woman replied with a smile. "You're the detective children, and your father owns The Trading Post."

"Yes, and we'd like to ask you a question," Pam went on. She told about the airplane they had seen on the meadow and added that they were double checking to see if it really was the minister's plane.

"That's our number, all right," Mrs. Wilkie replied. "But I'm afraid it was not my husband's plane. You see, he flew to California and has been there for the last week."

Pam's heart skipped a beat. *So! Just as she had suspected, the plane had false markings!*

"Thank you, Mrs. Wilkie," she said. "Good-by."

Mrs. Hollister headed back toward town. "Well, now you really have a fine clue!"

"Crickets," Pete said. "A plane with phony identification. That means trouble."

"For the pilot," Alex said.

"And for us, too," spoke up Dave. "How are we going to track it down?"

"Don't worry, it can be done," Pete declared.

Mrs. Hollister dropped Alex and Dave off at their homes before proceeding to the big house on Pine Lake.

While they waited for supper, the smaller children watched their favorite show on television. Ricky took his most comfortable position—elbows resting on the floor and the rest of him draped up and over the sofa.

"Ricky, your feet are touching the wall," Holly warned.

"Okay." He kicked off his shoes, which fell behind the furniture.

Pete and Pam, however, pulled up two chairs to the secretary desk and got out pads and pencils.

"Pete, do you think all of the original numbers were painted over and new ones put in?"

He bit on the end of his pencil for a few moments. "No. If the pilot did that, some people would be sure to spot the forgery."

"Well, then how—"

"I've got it! The faking could have been done with masking tape." Pete explained that by adding strips of white tape to the letters and numbers, they could be changed to look like something else.

"Then let's try to alter the figures in reverse," Pam suggested.

"That'll be quite a task, but it's our only hope." Pete recalled the advice that Officer Cal had given their detective club. Sleuthing, he had said, was not always glamorous. Often it took hours and hours of boring work.

First they considered the letter N. That could not be changed, because it meant U.S.A., and it was not likely that a small airplane could come across the ocean to Shoreham!

"Now take the two," Pete said. They both studied the numeral.

"It could be made from a one," the girl said.

"All right, let's put down one in place of two."

The six was another matter. Pete and Pam doodled on their pads, trying to come up with a substitute.

"Now I remember," Pam said excitedly. "There was a sort of a tail on the top of the six."

"Then maybe it was originally a five."

"Could be. Let's try it." They closed up the lower left side of a five until they had a six.

"That's our second number," Pete said. "You're doing great."

The eight, they decided, could easily have been a nine, if the bottom loop was completed. Now they had N159. But what about the remaining letters, which were AE?

"The A could be a number or a letter," Pete said. "What do you think, Pam?"

She closed her eyes and tried to recall the airplane that had whined past them in the evening darkness. All the letters were slanted to the right, she remembered, so that it would have been very easy to change the numeral one to an A.

"But that's just a guess," Pam said.

"I'll buy it. What about the final E?"

Pam sighed. "I'm getting cross-eyed working out this riddle!"

Pete snapped his fingers. "That's it. The owner of that plane probably felt the same way when he figured out the fake. Pam, let the E stand as it is."

The excited boy immediately phoned Mr. Pickett. Would he look up N1591E for them? Pete waited breathlessly for the results.

"Yes," said the man after a few moments. "There is such an airplane registration."

"Somebody around here?"

"No. The plane is owned and operated by the

Airterm Carrier Company, located at LaGuardia Airport in New York."

"Thank you," Pete said. "That's a big help, Mr. Pickett." He put down the phone and told the family.

"We're really hot on the trail, Pete!" Pam said. "Our mystery is nearly solved! And tonight Mr. Baker will tell us his big secret."

"I think he should know about this airplane number, too," Pete declared. He went to the phone and dialed. Luckily the investigator was in his room at the motel. He was amazed to hear about the latest clue.

"Does it help you any?" Pete asked.

"I'll say it does. Just the information we need!"

"Are you coming over and tell us your secret?"

"Yes. Later. And it will surprise you."

"See you, then," Pete said, and hung up. "He'll be over," he announced, "sometime after dinner."

Pam, who was busy helping her mother set the table, made a wry face when she heard this.

"What's the matter, Pam?" her mother asked. "You don't seem too keen about learning the secret."

"That's just it, Mother," her daughter replied. "Mr. Baker is going to tell us."

"Well?"

"We should tell him instead. That is, if we're real detectives."

At dinner everyone joined in the discussion about what the secret would be. There were lots of guesses. The silliest one came from Ricky, who thought that Mr. Chandar himself was the monster.

"We'll know soon," Mrs. Hollister said breezily, as she and her daughters cleared the table.

Mr. Hollister motioned toward the front lawn. Pete and Ricky knew immediately what he meant. On Friday evenings, if it wasn't raining, Pete would mow the lawn and Ricky would water his mother's flower garden.

The boys hastened outdoors. Soon the whine of the power mower was heard, and the clicking of the water meter indicated that Ricky was doing his duty to the snapdragons, petunias, and roses in his mother's garden.

When the chores were finished, Mrs. Hollister was called to the telephone and had a long talk with a friend. Pam beckoned to Holly and Sue. "Let's go in the other room and look at pictures."

"What kind?" Sue piped up. "Monsters?"

Pam went to the bookcase and pulled out several encyclopedias. Then she looked up some old *National Geographic* magazines. "We're going to learn about Borneo," she said.

Holly and Sue eagerly looked at the pictures that Pam spread before them. All three girls were intrigued by the colorful photos of the jungle island in the Malaysian chain.

"Oh, see these animals!" Sue chirped. There were monkeys and other creatures that looked something like apes.

"They're orangutans," Pam said. "It says here that they are so scarce that the people on Borneo don't allow anyone to take them from the country, except with special permission."

"What does that mean?" Holly asked.

Pam told her sister that hunters had killed so many orangutans that only a few thousand were left in the whole world.

"So they want to keep the orange-tans in Born-ee," Sue said. "Don't you see, Holly?"

The two younger girls studied the pictures, while Pam thumbed through the volume of her encyclopedia, numbered P. Soon she found what she was seeking.

Pongo. Pam gasped. *Pongo pygmaeus* was the name of the orangutan species. In the Malay language *orang* meant man, and *hutan,* forest. "Forest man," Pam whispered. "I've found it!" She clapped the book shut, and her face lit up with a big smile.

"Look, Pam's happy!" said Holly.

"You bet I am! Sue, Holly, I think I found the secret!" In whispered tones Pam explained that the monster mystery probably had something to do with an orangutan.

"Let's keep that a secret to ourselves," Holly suggested. "The boys think they're so smart!"

"I think I found the secret!"

Pam thought for a moment. "All right. Let's not say anything until I give the word."

Giggling, Holly and Sue ran into the yard and danced around Ricky, who was making loops in the air with the nozzle of the hose.

Zip, who happened to run in the way of the falling water, got all wet. The dog stood still and shook his fur. Drops splashed on the girls.

"Oh, Ricky, see what you did!" Holly declared, pulling on a damp pigtail.

"I didn't do anything, Zip did it!" Ricky protested.

"Just for that," said Sue, turning up her nose, "we won't tell you the secret."

Ricky dropped the hose and ran over to her. "Secret? Did you say secret?"

"Yes, she did," Holly said. "But we're not going to tell anybody! Not until Pam says so."

With that the two girls ran off, leaving Ricky to wonder what it was all about.

After the lawn had been cut and the garden watered, the Hollister children played tag for a while. Then, as the mosquitoes came out and lightning bugs flickered over the fresh-smelling lawn, they went indoors to wait for Mr. Baker.

An hour passed, and there was no sign of the investigator yet.

More time went by. "I'm afraid the little ones

will have to go to bed," Mrs. Hollister said. "You will hear about the secret in the morning."

"I have an idea, Mother," Pam spoke up. "I'll call Mr. Baker. Maybe he's on his way."

Pam telephoned the motel and talked to the clerk. Then she put down the phone and looked blankly at the others.

"He's not there!"

"Well, he must be coming," Mrs. Hollister said.

"No, Mother! Mr. Baker has checked out and left!"

CHAPTER 17

Up, Up, and Away!

"OH, DEAR," Mrs. Hollister said. "Something terrible must have happened."

Sue began to cry. "I hope nice Mr. Baker isn't a bad man," she sniffled.

"Of course he's not," Holly said stoutly.

"But I don't know about that Mr. Chandar," Ricky said, squinting his eyes.

"Didn't Mr. Baker leave any message at all?" asked their father.

"I didn't ask," Pam replied.

With that Pete went to the phone and called again.

"Yes," the clerk told him. "There is a message for the Hollisters."

"What does it say?" Pete asked excitedly.

"I don't know. It's in a sealed envelope."

"We'll be right over to get it," Pete said, and hung up.

Everyone clamored to go, but Mr. Hollister said,

"Pete and I will pick it up. You all stay here, just in case Mr. Baker should return."

They were at the motel in no time at all. Pete jumped out of the car, raced inside to get the envelope, thanked the clerk, and slid in again beside his father.

When they arrived home, Pete looked at the envelope. On the outside was written, "To the Hollister Family."

"Hurry, open it," begged Ricky.

Pete pulled out the letter.

"Read it!" Holly urged impatiently.

Pete began: *"Dear Hollisters, I know you will be disappointed, but I cannot tell you the secret tonight. I tried to telephone you, but your line was busy. Mr. Chandar and I have to return to New York immediately on very important business.*

"But we need your help. Could all of you, including your parents, come to Kennedy Airport tomorrow? There is a charter plane waiting for you at Shoreham Airport. You can return the same night. On arrival, come to my office in Federal Building 111. E. Baker, U. S. Game Management Agent."

"Yippee!" Ricky cried out loud. "We're going to New York!" He did a handspring on the rug, while Holly jumped up and down in excitement, her pigtails flying.

Pete and Pam looked at their parents. Mrs. Hollister was smiling, but their father had a worried look.

"What's the matter, Dad? Can't we go?" asked Pete.

His father replied that The Trading Post was having a big sale the next day. "I really should be there, Pete."

"But can't Indy Roades take charge?" Pam pleaded. "Tinker can help him." Tinker was a friendly older man who assisted at the store.

"It's Tinker's day off, and Indy would not be able to handle it alone."

"Why don't you ask Tinker if he'll postpone his holiday?"

Mr. Hollister went to the telephone and soon was talking to Tinker. He explained what had happened. Then he smiled. "Thanks. I know the children will appreciate it. I think they're finally going to solve the monster mystery."

As he hung up, Sue ran to her father and flung herself into his arms.

Suddenly Pete said, "You don't think this is all a big joke, do you, Dad?"

"You know how to find out. Phone the airport."

Pete did and was assured that Mr. Baker had indeed a chartered plane standing by to take the family to Kennedy Airport the next morning. It was a small executive jet, capable of flying nearly six hundred miles an hour.

When Pete hung up, he exclaimed, "Crickets! I've always wanted to fly in one of those! This will be a great adventure."

Next morning Sue and Holly gave the kittens milk and cat food. Pam fed Zip, while Pete saw that Domingo had a bagful of oats.

"Animals all set?" asked Mr. Hollister, as he backed the station wagon in front of the house.

"Yes, Daddy," Pam replied.

"Kids ready?"

"Here we are!" they chorused.

"Oh, I wonder what Mr. Baker wants us to do," Holly mused, as they drove to the airport.

"Maybe identify the airplane we saw in the meadow," Pete suggested.

When they reached the parking lot, everybody got out and hastened into the terminal. There they were met by a smiling young man in a pilot's uniform. He counted heads and laughed. "You must be the Hollisters—seven of you!"

Mr. Hollister confirmed this and introduced the family.

"I'm Harry Sturges. Follow me." The pilot led them to a beautiful, sleek, white airplane. They climbed up steps in front, and the pilot locked the door. The motors began, and the plane whistled across the runway.

"Yikes!" Ricky said. He put his hands to his ears

and rolled his eyes. "That's what I want to be when I grow up—a jet pilot."

"Up, up, and away," sang Pam.

Before they knew it, the Hollisters were high in the air. To while away the time, Mrs. Hollister pulled a piece of string from her purse and played cat's cradle with Sue.

Soon they were looking down on the busy runways of Kennedy International Airport. The plane landed and taxied to a private hangar, where a limousine was waiting for them. They thanked the pilot and piled in.

Federal Building 111, they found, was at the outer fringes of the airport, not far from the super highways which snaked across Long Island.

Their chauffeur parked, led them into the building, and down one long corridor. They turned a corner, descended a few steps, and came before a huge basement room. The chauffeur knocked on the door, opened it, and announced, "The Hollisters are here, Mr. Baker."

The tall government man rose from behind his desk. He had been chatting with Mr. Chandar. Now he greeted his guests and introduced the Indonesian to Mr. and Mrs. Hollister. Then Mr. Baker's secretary brought chairs for everyone. When they were seated, the tall man began, "I have a surprise for all of you. That monster which has been scaring Shoreham is really a—"

"An orange tang!" Sue piped up. She put her hand to her mouth and giggled.

The two investigators looked at each other, amazed. "You—you know?" Mr. Chandar asked.

"We guessed it," Pam said, and told how they had put the clues together.

Pete and Ricky, who were not in on the girls' secret, just looked at each other, open-mouthed.

"Maybe you'll be a monkey's uncle," said Holly.

Mr. Baker's deep laughter filled the room. "An orangutan's uncle, that's more like it."

Sue giggled even louder.

"Well, wait till you hear the rest of the story," Mr. Baker went on, and told the Hollisters that some wild animals in the world were in danger of extinction.

"And among those are the orangs," Holly spoke up. "Pam read it to us in the encyclopedia."

"Right. Others are grizzly bears, wolves, gazelles, Galapagos tortoises, pygmy hippos, and bald eagles. All these are on the endangered list."

"Yikes!" said Ricky. "I guess the bald eagles are kind of old, anyway."

Mr. Baker smiled. "The orangutans," he went on, "are about the scarcest of all and soon might die out."

"That's why they are not allowed to be taken out of Borneo," Mr. Chandar spoke up. "Borneo is my country, you know."

"What brought you over here?" Pete inquired.

"I'm a private detective. You see, a little girl I know named Subu had two pet orangs. They were twin babies."

"How cute!" Sue interrupted. "How did she get them?"

"Her father found them in the woods after someone had killed the mother."

"Oh, no!" Pam exclaimed. "How could anyone be so cruel?"

"Well, the hunters were probably after the babies, but they had to kill the mother first to get them. Anyway, one of the babies was kidnaped and taken to Shanghai. From there it was flown to the United States by a gang of animal smugglers."

"Animal smugglers?" Pete asked, surprised.

"Yes. Since these rare animals cost a lot of money, animal smuggling has become a big racket."

Mr. Baker nodded, then he smiled. "So you see, Mr. Chandar was not a bad man, as you thought in the beginning. He was only looking for Pongo."

"Is that the baby orange tang's name?" Sue asked.

"Yes. And his twin is called Bongo." Mr. Chandar explained that little Subu had become ill with worry over Pongo, and the twin Bongo would not eat. "That's why I was sent here, to find Pongo."

"Now we are after this gang of smugglers," Mr. Baker explained. "When we heard about a monster in Shoreham, we figured that their hide-out was nearby and that perhaps one of the kidnaped animals had escaped."

"That's sure some mystery," Mr. Hollister said. "You kids really stumbled into a big one."

"Yes, and it has helped the United States Government a lot," Mr. Baker said.

Now the Hollister children were full of questions about orangutans.

"Do they eat eggs?" asked Pam.

"Yes," Mr. Chandar replied. "They love eggs. They also eat bananas and bark and leaves."

"Now we know who took Mrs. Elder's eggs and Mrs. Kane's pudding," Holly giggled. "Poor little Pongo was hungry."

Mr. Chandar added that orangs live in tree platforms built in the highest branches. "They're very smart creatures," he said, "and cover themselves with leaves when it rains."

"Then it was Pongo's nest you were looking at?" Pete asked. "The one we saw in the tall pine tree?"

The Indonesian admitted that he had watched the tree house for a long time, even caught a glimpse of the orang once and chased him along the lake front. But Pongo had escaped him.

Sue and Holly laughed. "So you were the one who was running after that little boy!" Holly said.

"Little boy?"

"Well, we thought it was a little boy, but it was

really Pongo," Holly explained. "He also must have been the one who looked into our basement window."

"But what about those funny footprints?" Ricky spoke up. "They didn't look like an orang's."

"I have no answer to that," Mr. Chandar said. "Perhaps they were tampered with by the smugglers to create the impression that it was really a monster which haunted Shoreham."

"Well, so much for that," Mr. Baker said finally, looking very serious. "Now we have another problem. Mr. Chandar just received a cable from Borneo, saying that little Bongo has also been kidnaped."

"He was probably taken by the same smuggling gang," Mr. Chandar put in.

"How terrible!" Mrs. Hollister said. "Do you expect him to be flown to New York, too?"

"I think Bongo may already be in the United States," Mr. Baker said. "While I was away, I had an assistant take pictures of all the animals brought to this airport and of the people who picked them up." He reached into a drawer and pulled out a photo. It showed a man standing beside a cage.

The Hollisters rose from their chairs and crowded around the government agent.

Holly shrieked. "That's the man we saw in the school!"

"Are you sure?" Mr. Baker asked.

"Sure," said Sue. "He was in the toy library."

"That's the man we saw!" Holly shrieked.

"Then he's the one of the gang who has head-quarters in or near Shoreham," Mr. Baker reasoned. "But what was he doing in the toy library?"

"Looking for Pongo!" Holly declared. "Maybe the poor little orang baby had entered the school through an open window!"

They studied the picture longer. The cage which the strange man was claiming was marked "Live Red Monkey."

"That's what the crooks do sometimes," Mr. Baker went on. "They say that the orangs are monkeys, and there are plenty of monkeys!"

"How can you tell the difference?" Mr. Hollister asked.

"The orangs have naked ears and thin, reddish hair. In addition, their hands have long fingers with a very small, stumpy thumb."

"Where is this man now?" Pete wanted to know.

"His plane is based at LaGuardia Airport," Mr. Baker said. "That's why I wanted you to come—to identify the craft."

Mr. Chandar said that the crate more than likely contained Bongo and no doubt was to be smuggled to the Shoreham hide-out.

"Let's get over to LaGuardia right away," Mr. Baker suggested. They all followed him out to the back of the building. A helicopter was waiting, and they climbed inside.

The rotors whirled, and soon they were flying

across Long Island to the North Shore. The rows of apartments below looked like toy buildings. After the helicopter had landed, Mr. Baker hailed a government station wagon, which took them to another private hangar.

"I've had the airplane located," he explained. "It's right in here."

The Hollisters tingled with excitement as Mr. Baker marched into a door marked "Office." He returned with a man in a white coverall and ordered him to raise the hangar doors. At first the man protested, then shrugged and did what he was told.

The doors opened. *Nothing was inside!*

"Where did that plane go?" Mr. Baker demanded.

"I don't know," the attendant replied.

"Was there something else in it besides the pilot?"

"Yes. A couple of crates with animals. I didn't see what kind."

Mr. Baker turned to the Hollisters. "I'm sure he went to Shoreham. We must hurry; there's not a moment to lose!"

CHAPTER 18

The Spooky Gate

THE helicopter took the Hollisters back to Mr. Baker's office, where plans were quickly laid to catch the animal smugglers.

"The single-engine plane is not too fast," Pete said. "We could be in Shoreham long before that thief arrives."

"You say he landed at dusk before?" Mr. Baker asked.

"It was nearly dark," Pam said.

"Then he'll try to do the same thing again, I'm sure. He'll probably stop somewhere in between here and Shoreham. Well, when he gets there, he'll have a real reception, this time."

Now all of them, including Mr. Chandar, returned to the private jet, where the smiling pilot was waiting for them.

"Back to Shoreham," Mr. Baker said, as the Hollisters scampered up the stairway and into the cabin. Once they were air-borne, Mr. Chandar told the youngsters about life in Indonesia. "Someday you must visit my country," he said.

"Oh, yes. I'd like to meet Subu," Holly piped up.

"Me, too," declared Sue. "And we could play with orangutans, couldn't we?"

"Hooray! She said it right!" Ricky exclaimed. "Now you're almost as smart as I am."

Sue made a face at her brother. All of a sudden her stomach began to feel funny, as the jet descended toward Shoreham Airport, and she sat very still until they had touched ground.

After the landing the passengers said good-by to the pilot, and Mr. Hollister led the procession to the station wagon. "First stop, police headquarters, I would think," he said, looking at Mr. Baker.

"Right. Now we set the trap for these rascals."

Officer Cal was at his office when they arrived. He and the police chief praised the detective work that had gone on.

Then plans were made. The police, with the assistance of some state troopers, would stake out the park area. "There'll be people around the meadow," Officer Cal said. "We'll let the plane land, then grab the pilot."

"Oh, I do hope he lands with Bongo," Pam said.

"Officer Cal," Pete asked, "will you come with us to that old mine shaft? I'm sure something's going to happen up there, too."

At a nod from the chief, the young policeman said, "All right, boys. We'll check it out after supper. Meet me here at seven."

Excitement in the Hollister home flickered like summer lightning. Hardly anyone had an appetite for the hamburger and hot dog cookout, to which Alex Kane and Dave Mead had been invited. The children just nibbled and looked at each other with wide grins, anticipating the arrival of the smugglers' airplane.

"Crickets! That guy doesn't know what he's getting into," Pete said.

"Do you suppose that there's some other man involved in this?" Alex asked.

"There has to be," Pam spoke up. "Or else who would take care of the animals in their hide-out?"

Everybody wanted to be in on the final action, but the older children realized that this was not possible. It was agreed that Mrs. Hollister and Sue would remain in the station wagon, parked near the park entrance. Mr. Hollister and Holly would join two state troopers spying on the meadow.

Ricky, Pete, Pam, Alex, and Dave would show Officer Cal to the place where the spooky gate covered the old mine shaft.

All of them brought walkie-talkies when they drove to headquarters. From there they rode to the park in three police cars.

The daylight had begun to fade, and the green

meadow was observed by the sharp eyes of the police. The boys and Pam climbed the steep cliff and led Officer Cal past the place where their knapsacks had disappeared, to the mine shaft.

When they reached the iron bars, the policeman put his ear close to the opening and listened. "I think you're right. Something's stirring inside there!"

"I'll report to Dad over the walkie-talkie," Pete said, and spoke into his radio. As he did, there was a slight click in the iron bars. Suddenly they began to sink into the ground! The black mouth of the cave gaped wide open!

Everyone gasped. "Dave, you were right!" Pete whispered.

"How'd it open?" Alex asked, trying to suppress the chill that ran down his spine.

"I think I know," Officer Cal said. "That walkie-talkie activated an electronic device to operate these bars. Somebody is using this for a hide-out."

The policeman explained that once he had been broadcasting from his prowl car and the garage doors of houses in the neighborhood had suddenly lifted up. "So I know it's possible."

"Of course!" Pete exclaimed. "That's what must have happened to Mr. Messina's garage door, too."

Officer Cal pulled a large flashlight from his hip and beamed it into the tunnel.

"Ohhh! Look at that!" Ricky quavered, as two

eyes glowed in the dark. Then there was a scampering of hoofs.

"Watch out!" Officer Cal called. The children jumped back. Out of the cave charged the smallest hippo they had ever seen. Quickly Pete grabbed the animal's head and Alex held tight to his back hoofs. Using their cliff-scaling rope, they hog-tied the frightened little animal.

Next came an orangutan.

"It must be Pongo!" Pam cried out. She reached for the animal's hand. It leaped onto her, throwing its arms around the girl's neck.

Suddenly a man raced out of the tunnel.

"Halt!" shouted Officer Cal. The man looked wildly about, the powerful light shining in his eyes. Before he knew what was happening, the policeman had snapped handcuffs on him.

"Yikes, we got one of 'em!" Ricky shouted.

While the boys now clung to the prisoner, Officer Cal stepped inside and shone his light about the cage. Before he reached the perpendicular drop of the old mine shaft, he found a large room cut in the hill.

In it were remnants of food, a table and bench, and in a corner a tub with water. Rags were thrown on the ground. "Probably for the animals to sleep on," the policeman thought, shaking his head.

He went back to the entrance. "There's nothing more in the cave," he reported. "Let's put the ani-

"Watch out!" Officer Cal called.

mals back there for the time being and go down to the meadow."

The boys helped him put the two little creatures back into the mine shaft, and locked the gate. Then Officer Cal quickly led the way, taking their prisoner with him. They took a detour around the cliff, since they had left their rope in the cave, but soon reached Officer Cal's car, which was parked at the bottom. Then they drove back to the meadow.

There the criminal was handed over to two policemen, and Officer Cal and the children took their places behind a clump of bushes on the grassy plain.

Soon the sound of an airplane filled the evening sky.

"It's coming! It's coming!" Ricky shouted, and the children looked on, fascinated, as the craft's running lights appeared. Then a bright landing light flooded the area. The craft touched down and taxied to the edge of the woods nearly in front of the youngsters. Presently the engine stopped.

In the gloom, the cabin door opened and a man stepped out onto the ground. Everything was silent. "Nip!" the man called. "Nip, are you there? I've got the other twin. The pair should be worth a fortune."

Across the meadow, Pete could make out several shadowy figures stealing quietly toward the plane.

"Lay low, all of you," Officer Cal commanded. "This man may be armed."

The children flattened themselves on the ground, while Cal Newberry walked toward the airplane. When the pilot saw him, he said, "So there you are, Nip. Right on time."

Suddenly the smuggler realized that it was not his confederate. With a cry of alarm he tried to get back into the plane. Officer Cal made a dive for him but missed. The pilot rolled over on the ground right under the plane and sprang up on the other side.

"Come on, fellows," Pete ordered. "Let's get him!" The boys darted from hiding and streaked toward the fugitive as he headed to the woods.

Pete tackled one leg, Alex the other. Dave and Ricky jumped on the man's back.

Blam! The smuggler fell to the ground, stunned.

"We got him!" Ricky cried out.

"Officer Cal! Over this way!" Pete shouted.

The fellow struggled, but it was no use. The boys clung to him, and Ricky sat on his head as Officer Cal ran up to them.

"Okay, fellows, leave him to me."

The boys released their captive. The policeman collared him and pulled him to his feet, shining the light full on the man's face.

He was the one who had claimed the crate marked "Live Red Monkey"!

By this time running feet came from across the meadow, and the airplane was quickly surrounded by the police. Holly stood nearby, holding her father's hand and shaking with excitement. Mr. Baker and Mr. Chandar came up with long strides.

Officer Cal turned the pilot over to two tall policemen, then he and the two investigators searched the aircraft.

They found a box marked "Live Red Monkey." Mr. Baker opened it.

"Just as I thought, an orangutan," he commented.

"It's Bongo!" Mr. Chandar exclaimed. "See that little red chain around his left leg?"

The animal recognized his name and reached out his arms toward the man, who took him out of the plane.

By this time floodlights illuminated the meadow.

"Oh, I wish Mother could see that!" Pam said.

"Why don't you go back and get her," Mr. Hollister said. "Meet us right here."

Fifteen minutes later, just as the police had finished examining the airplane, Mrs. Hollister arrived with Sue.

"Is this Pongo?" the little girl asked, sleepily rubbing her eyes.

Mr. Chandar smiled. "No, it's his twin, Bongo."

"I know where Pongo is," cried Pete. "Let's go back to the old mine shaft!"

The Hollisters piled into the station wagon, and

the two investigators drove with Officer Cal in his prowl car. They parked at the bottom of the cliff and climbed up the rest of the way. When they arrived at the cave, Officer Cal opened the iron gate. The other orang hopped up toward them.

Mr. Chandar looked at the animal, then said sadly, "This is not Pongo. He's much larger."

The children's faces dropped.

"The tree house!" Alex cried out. "Let's go over to the tree house!"

They could only drive part of the way, but it did not take too long before they reached the tall pine tree. There was no sign of life in the nest above.

"I have an idea," Mr. Chandar said. He took Bongo and placed him on the tree trunk. When the searchlight was shone to the top, Bongo ran up quickly, then his head disappeared in the tree house.

Moments later those on the ground heard a cry of delight, and two little heads peered over the side of the nest!

"Pongo and Bongo! They're together!" Pam cried, and the children jumped up and down with joy.

"I wonder who the other one is, the one we left in the cave with the little hippo," Alex mused.

"Perhaps he belongs to another child in Borneo," Dave said.

"We'll have to pick those two up later," Officer Cal said, "and if we can't find their owners, they'll be given to a zoo. Hey, look out there!" he suddenly warned.

Just then something flew out of the tree house and came hurtling to the ground. It was followed by two more dark objects. *Thud! Thud! Thud!*

"Our knapsacks!" Pete exclaimed.

"So that's where they were!" Dave said. "Pongo discovered them in the woods and took them!"

"Probably trying to find something to eat," Mrs. Hollister said with a smile.

Then Mr. Chandar began to call to the orangutan twins in a quiet, soothing voice. They stepped off the tree house and began backing toward the ground.

"Aren't they cute," Sue said.

"And all the time we thought Pongo was a monster!" Dave Mead grinned.

"Now I know who made those footprints!" Pete suddenly snapped his fingers. "Remember the police chief thought part of it looked like a small hippo? They were made by two animals, the little hippo, which must have escaped once, too, and Pongo together!"

"Either that, or there might even be another hippo running lose in Shoreham," Alex reasoned.

As the two animals were about to jump to the

ground, the Hollisters suddenly noticed a large object in Pongo's arm.

"Oh, no!" Pam cried out. "Look, Mother, it's the Viennese doll!"

"So Pongo really was at the toy library," her mother said, chuckling. "I guess that solves the mystery."

All seemed jolly, except Ricky, who looked rather glum. "Yikes, but what about the monster I saw on the lake?"

Just then the police received a report over their walkie-talkie. The two criminals were in jail and confessing.

"One of them said that a Galapagos turtle got away from them," Officer Cal said. "So did the little hippo, but they caught it again."

"So that was it!" Pete declared. "The turtle got into Pine Lake, and that's what you saw, Ricky!"

The redhead gulped, grinned, and bobbed his head up and down. "Monster, schmonster," he said. "Do we have something to tell Joey Brill!"